Second of a Four Book Set

Part I   *10000 Meals*
Part II   *20 Years of New Earth*
Part III   *The Diaries of Terri and Mia Johnson*
Part IV   *The Holiday of Pie Johnson*

Published by:

Classic Publishers

ISBN: 978-1-941263-08-2

Heat

It was called the water transformer. A silly looking contraption. The best description would be an oversized water faucet with a spigot about two feet wide. Instead of being connected to pipes, the back had an open bowl bolted on back, ten feet wide with air rushing inside. Operation of the machine was easy to explain. The planet Lanny Fillmore had landed on was completely barren of H_2O. Not a single drop. But the air, injected with the slightest touch of a unique electrical charge, was packed with hydrogen and oxygen, necessary components for creating H_2O – water if you will. The water transformer provided a simple catalyst that, using the electrical charge in the air as its energy source, merged hydrogen and oxygen molecules to form water. The catalyst was attached to several metallic slats inside the water transformer. The device was designed to draw air into the open bowl, pushing through the massive spigot. As the hydrogen and oxygen molecules rushed past, they would come in contact with the catalyst, converting into water, which would pour out the faucet at the other end.

Once expelled, the water would sink into the ground, which as far as the eye could see was a blanket of what looked like mounds of oversized packaging Styrofoam popcorn, gold in color and containing a mix of nutrients along with more hydrogen and oxygen.

The theory was, as the water transformer deposited water into the metallic like golden shavings, the H_2O would interact with the golden kernels, turning the shavings into an extremely fertile paste, spewing off watery steam as a byproduct. The problem was, the water transformer was working, a loud whoosh of air blowing through its inner mechanisms… but nothing had come out. Nothing but air that is, hot air. The directions stated that first a heavy steam would appear at the tap, followed by a misty rain. Then finally water, pure and clean, would flow from the large spigot.

The water transformer had been in operation for over a week with no results and Lanny, once so happy to have survived the trip to New Earth, was becoming concerned. The rocket ship had been packed with enough food for the three year trip from Earth, but only barely. As a precaution, Lanny had done well conserving his supplies, but he was down to his last stack of food and if the vegetable seeds didn't take, he was a dead man. To plant seeds, he needed water and some sort of dirt. It was bad enough daytime temperatures reached a hundred forty plus, dropping at night to negative forty, forcing him inside his spacecraft except for the a short periods of time during daylight and nightfall when the weather was more temperate. He had already burned his hand once putting it under the huge spigot – which felt like a huge hair dryer – and had yet to see the first sign of a drop of water. But wasn't that a good sign? The hand being burned that is. Didn't that mean… even though he didn't see it, steam was pouring out of the tap?

As for checking out his surroundings, the small steel shards laying all about kept him from any real venturing about, not that there was anything to see. The report from the computer before landing implied the planet was similar to Earth, with a molten core surrounding a solid crust. But as for the yellow – hard and sharp – shavings that covered everything, he didn't know if it they were a yard deep or a hundred miles. From what he had seen, they apparently covered the entire planet.

That was what all he had puzzled out from the original landing and a few short trips taken in his ship. One thing that was plentiful was energy – in the form of fuel on his rocket ship. But what good was that, when the only thing to see were rugged hard golden nuggets that weren't even made of gold, with razor sharp points on them? The instructions said to be patient. That there was so much hydrogen and oxygen in the air, it might all turn to steam for a day or two. But it was going on a week, and starting a second, and that didn't make sense anyway. What he needed was water, and some dirt… and some decent weather. None of which had been experienced since arrival. No clouds, or smog… no nothing. Just blistering heat with a pure blue sky in the day and biting cold in the dark of night, with a few survivable hours in between.

He had done some small experiments with his water. Not much, but he did risk a little of his precious supply. Putting some of the golden shards in a bowl, he poured a spot of water on them. Sure enough, the nuggets turned to a pasty mush while steam billowed off. And then? The planted tomato seed had already started to grow, and quickly at that. But here was the problem. He only had so much water. If he used water on making food, he'd have none to drink.

The water transformer was supposed to make enough water to quickly form a small oasis where he could live. Again, that was in the instructions. Obviously that hadn't happened. If he planted everything in his cramped rocket ship, what was he supposed to do when he ran out of room? As Lanny saw it, that was a starvation diet. For now he was holding onto his precious stock of seeds, hoping the water transformer would improve its output. Some *damn water* to be specific. Even a drop would be a good sign.

According to the readings inside the rocket ship, the temperature outside was a hundred twenty when he went to check on the water transformer, and dropping. Apparently the temperature maintained either at the high all day or the low at night. In the short time between of temperature change, and he could escape the ship, greeted only by the hiss of the air blasting through the water transformer.

Returning inside he read the instructions once more. One or two days of steam. A half week to a week of water droplets. And then... a small stream of water that would increase every day until the entire diameter of the two foot wide tap was pumping out healthy water, providing dirt for plants, cooling off the days, and creating drinkable fluids.

What a pile of crap. Maybe if he knew more about the process, like those geniuses that were supposed to be making this trip. Was he doing something wrong? He'd checked the water transformer and checked it again. No moving parts, just some black slats inside that were supposed to cause the chemical reaction that would bring the hydrogen and oxygen together. Not even some moving parts to suck the air past. A worthless piece of junk. It didn't work, but someone made money selling it to the US Government, who paid a pretty penny for it. Suckers. He'd of been better off on Earth waiting with his family for SS 222.

But then reality sunk in. Earth was dying and he knew that. The huge rip in the Earth's crust was the end for that planet. Even though the water transformer didn't have any moving parts, air howled through it day and night. Something was causing that, so they had that part right. Staring at the blizzard of stars in popping up in the evening sky, Lanny grimly told himself, it was time to grow up. He'd been spoiled his whole life, and had taken full advantage. But now? If he didn't get this water making contraption running, he was dead.

Is It A Drop?

It started like any other day, or night. Complete failure, with only the shrinking of his food stores to show the passage of time. Preparing to return inside the ship as morning as temperatures passed one hundred thirty, he heard a sizzle. Or did he? It was hard to hear anything over the constant whoosh of the water transformer. The sound was enough to stop Lanny, waiting to make sure he had heard something. After a pause there was a second sizzle. Were he able to, he'd have run back, but the golden kernels under his feet had already shown they would slice his shoes to bits if he did so.

Returning slowly... there was another, and then another. Arriving, he saw a drip quiver on lip of the tap, before falling, landing on the ground with another sizzle. He stood immobile for five minutes, earning nothing for his efforts. Scooping up where the drops apparently had landed, he returned to the rocket ship to investigate. Sure enough, some of the shavings had indentations as if water had landed on them, melting away the roughness, and leaving the tiniest remnants of a mushy paste.

That evening he rushed out to see… nothing. No water, no droplets, no mush. To keep his spirits up, he ate the tiny tomato that had grown from the seed, thinking it might be the last vegetable he ever ate. Depressed as he was, he still found himself excited the next morning as the sun began to rise. Ignoring the biting cold, Lanny pushed out to the water transformer, and waited. Sure enough, he spied a drop of water, forming on the lip of the tap. Flicking a finger on it, he then dabbed his tongue on the wet spot. Never had water tasted better. Staying outside as long as he could, he observed the minute improvement in water production with his watch, first a drop falling every fifteen minutes, then every ten, then every five. By the time peak temperatures hit, the water transformer produced a drop almost every two minutes. By evening he was again the picture of disappointment, the unsteady stream of drops a distant memory, leaving Lanny to again wait for morning.

After a fitful sleep he awoke to a steady drip-drip-drip of water sinking into the ground, congealing the hard nuggets into a dirt like goo, and by the time he had to return to the safety of his rocket to escape the heat, it was with a small cup of hot water. That was his drink for dinner, the food almost gone except for some green tomatoes on the verge of turning ripe. He had more planted… some beans as well, having just started those, peeing on them for water.

With morning came a steady dribble of water and some riper tomatoes. It seems the ground was ideal for farming. Over the course of the next week every day was a relative joy, the amount of water increasing daily from the spigot, getting as thick as his wrist, disappearing into the ground, sending steam into the air. He had enough of the mushy ground to make a path to the rocket and packed the rocket's insides with the newly created dirt, used to plant peanuts, potatoes, and onions.

With the food supply down to the last few frozen meals, he now existed on water, more water, and a little bits of vegetables as they became edible. The spigot continued to increase in water flow, reaching a width as thick as his arm, then leg, then waist, pushing towards expanding to the full measure of the tap's width during the daytime hours.

The flow of water became enough that Lanny awoke the next morning to a small pond forming outside his ship. Previously the water disappeared into the golden nuggets, sending off a spray of steam. But today, a small slip of water, maybe ten feet wide, with the hiss of water vapor around him announcing the hard crunching balls were converting to fertile land. As it expanded, every so often a break in the bottom of his small lake would cause a whirlpool of water leaking out the hole created as it soaked into the ground, blasts of steam pushing their way to the surface. Then, as the hole patched itself with newly created dirt, the now almost empty puddle began to refill with water from the spigot.

As more water poured out, the shallow puddle began expanding. Where was the rest going? Seeping deep into the bed of golden kernels was the best guess. With the onset of night the pond quickly froze over. Rather than be frustrated, Lanny found himself outside slipping about on his small rink, laughing at the joy of such a simple task despite the cool temperatures.

Physically he was starving, wasting away, his potatoes and peanuts taking forever to mature. In a bit of desperation some of the seeds were planted outside, ringing the small pond, now thirty feet across. He had little hope for them with the extreme heat and cold, but something had to be done. And though he couldn't bring the ship's temperature gauge to the pond, he was sure that around his small pool, it was cooler during the day, and warmer at night. The first set of planting was a waste, as was the second. Simply too cold at night.

More dirt was crammed into the small ship and the remainder of his seeds were planted. A few tomatoes wouldn't keep him alive for long. To keep his spirits up, he took to splashing about in his pond in the mornings, as it expanded to fifty feet across and several feet deep. He only had so long before the water heated to the point it was no longer safe. But he noticed every day, as the lake expanded, the water stayed temperate longer and longer and he had to wait longer for the pond to ice over.

There are bad problems and good ones. Lanny considered the fact the pond was growing into a tiny lake threatening to overwhelm his rocket ship a good problem. The ship, beginning to malfunction from too much dirt in the vents, was started and transported to the top of the highest berm of golden nuggets he could find near the growing lake, bringing the water transformer along. Much to Lanny's surprise, the small area around the lake was becoming more hospitable, with daytime temperatures by the water peaking at one ten to one twenty. Still very hot, but certainly survivable. And at night? It was a bracingly cold negative twenty. But a twenty degree increase was promising.

The good news was followed with more, as the small lake breached the shore line and started a small river downstream. How far would it flow wondered Lanny. The rocket ship he had arrived on one of two recommended landing spots. One was a large mesa of land at about ten thousand feet above what could be considered sea level... that is if there were seas with water in them. This first of highland was about a hundred fifty to two hundred miles wide and eight hundred miles long from north to south. The second was another mesa beside the first. Between the two large plateaus was a five thousand foot mostly sheer rock face, with areas where the rock had broken into a gentle slope. The second mesa was two hundred miles wide and a thousand miles long north to south. Lanny had selected the lower mesa, but with no basis to make such a decision. As Lanny thought, "Hey, you gotta make a call." For convenience he dropped the ship about halfway between the north and south ends of the plain and near the cliff that separated the two expanses.

Below the lower mesa was a wide open valley basin with another sheer wall separating them, with no breaks that would allow an easy path to the bottom.

With the rocket ship placed near the cliff wall to the first mesa, Lanny watched every day in fascination as his river slowly meandered toward the second ledge and the valley basin below. It was a slow process, with the river expanding maybe a foot a day, steam bellowing out at the edges as water converted the land from barren nuggets to fertile and more hospitable dirt. As time went on, it seemed some of the moist air remained captured in the hollow where Lanny had landed, and after a while, the edges of the lake slowly started to turn to mush, as the lake became deep enough that even in the coldest of nights it didn't freeze over.

One day, to Lanny's surprise, the impossible happened. Near the lake where some of the gold nuggets had turned to mush, a few of the seeds tossed into the ground began to grow. The rocket ship had been supplied with a fifty pound bag of desert grass seed, and handfuls were dumped around the lake. Sure enough, they took and began to grow. With the arrival of small tufts of green, the temperature again improved in the daytime, possibly to the low hundreds – just around the lake that is. A few feet from the water, New Earth was as hostile as when Lanny arrived. At night? Still an amazingly cold negative ten just a few feet outside the protective forces of the lake. And ten feet away? No different than when he first arrived.

These encouraging signs were enough for Lanny to seed around the lake and even beside the slowly growing river. The days were no longer spent in his rocket playing video games, nor splashing about in the water. Now he was a grass farmer, pushing and shoving water in all directions, trying to bring temperatures even further within the range of the planet he had left behind.

The second wave of grass seeds took and he began to strategically plant vegetables, selecting areas where the grass grew thickest and greenest, hoping they might provide protection to the plants. The plan was a success, assisted by pieces of clothing used to cover the plants at night. Finally one night in his sleep, a thought occurred to him. As he slept, his mind calculated and recalculated the growth of the water on the ground, the amount of vegetables growing, and what was needed to survive. There was enough. He was able to properly feed himself. Soon old and unused fruit was tossed into the river where the seeds washed down the short straight of water to the hissing end where the river continued its steady steamy path of growth – still growing about a foot a day.

With the knowledge he had succeeded, Lanny found a great depression coming over him. Two ships, SS 221 and SS 222 were supposed to be arriving on this planet, but he had left two years ahead of them. Now he was confident of survival, how would he make it through the time needed to wait for them? He'd already suffered three years alone crammed into a tiny rocket ship. How long would it be before he saw another human face? That was assuming they managed to make it. The switch to the seventh dimension had almost torn his ship apart. What would it do with the much larger space stations… stocked with people, animals, and who knows what else. If they could make it to the seventh dimension, then it was possible they might make it to the planet. But that brought another problem. His small craft had been designed to handle the descent to New Earth. How would that work with a weighted down four hundred foot long space station? The landing had been rough for Lanny, and he couldn't imagine it would be any better for a craft as long as a sky scraper.

That was a problem for another day. For now, he was surviving. No… better than that, he was thriving, at least compared to his arrival. Sleep came easier and food was abundant. As for having some company? It would be nice, but with a full belly and improving weather, he was doing alright.

Preparations For Liftoff

XJ2 was jammed, wedged between SS 222 and XJ4, the rocket ship Gordon had arrived on with his family. The slight rotation of the space station was keeping pressure on XJ2 to remain in place. This was the first assigned task assigned to Captain Majewski as the official captain of SS 222. To properly and safely remove XJ2, and secure it to SS 222. By all accounts, the Captain succeeded and quite well. The original specifications for SS 222 had called for all four of the XJ rockets to be attached evenly around the space station. They were to be locked down securely, giving additional weight and protection to the space station in flight before providing assistance with the descent into New Earth using their reverse thrusters and opening a host of parachutes concealed inside.

But with XJ1 disappearing into the distance, and XJ3 destroyed on the launch pad, the originally planned formation was no longer possible. The logical solution was to attach the two remaining rocket ships, XJ2 and XJ4, on opposite sides of the space station. Hopefully they would balance each other out. The theory was logical, but there was no way to replace the lost reverse thrusters from XJ1 and XJ3, nor their parachutes.

Still, the mood onboard was upbeat when, through careful maneuvering, the captain freed XJ2, positioning and securing it properly in the docking area. Adding to the good vibe was the treasure trove of wealth found inside. There were a few calls to toss the gold and other valuables overboard, labeling the property blood money. But these complaints were cast aside by Jim LaBlanc, who wasted no time in acting as the small community's informal City Manager. Not elected, nor the leader, but rather making sure everything on the ship worked as is should and that the ship's attitude was positive. He determined tossing off such treasures act of bitterness, and would add nothing to the task ahead. These items could be used as prizes, gifts given out to those who worked hard toward the community and success of the mission. Or possibly these items, that held no value right now, might be life saving objects on their destination planet.

As for the unofficial leaders, Gordon, Terri, and Captain Majewski were eager to keep their triumvirate active, and Jim made no attempts to dismantle it. After all, he had Dolly, who slid into the informal role of royalty on the ship. If ever he wanted to make a change, he was sure that with Dolly's backing, the necessary changes could be made.

But why make any alteration? The triumvirate seemed for the most part to be treating everyone fairly, and wasn't that what really mattered? As for the additional bodies on board? Those over the two hundred and ten that were approved. A more exacting review of the amount of food on board had been completed and yes, it would be tight, very much so. When Captain Majewski became upset over that fact, reminding everyone they had taken on too many passengers, Jim simply requested a list of those the Captain wanted to kill... nothing more was said on the subject. SS 222 would move forward with its current complement of passengers, for better or worse.

The bodies of the dead were transferred from the dining room to the freezers where they were tagged and stored. After all, you didn't want children eating their parents, although such words upset Terri, who commented, "And who would you like them to eat?" Jim knew that was the right thing to do. Years from now, he wanted anyone who asked to know, everyone had been treated with respect and honor, or as much as could be afforded in such an insane situation.

The other immediate concern was the docking area ripped apart when XJ1 had slammed into it. A space suit was found on XJ2, an old service workers uniform with a leak. But once repaired and made functional, Gordon and a few of the techs were able to take short jaunts outside, sealing the hole. Although it was no longer a serviceable room, once finished, there was confidence it would make the trip to New Earth.

As for Kevin and the Senator's ex girlfriend? Failure. She found Kevin smug and self centered while he... well he *was* smug and self centered. He found her lack of a degree off-putting and she thought his lack of understanding of People magazine made him boring.

Barry had taken over as informal head of security, or as they joked in their meetings, truant officer. He roved about ship at all hours as if ready to hit someone on a moment's notice. It was annoying, but Jim understood that even in outer space, security was needed. Food was meted out tightly, with the thin chef assigned the role of cook. Not that he wanted the position, but someone had to cut up, grind, and serve the human remains as food. That was his job and why he was on board. That he disapproved? Jim didn't care. In fact he didn't care for the thin chef at all, who turned out to be a complainer, always with a problem that no one could solve.

There was one item Jim refused to waver on. Education. The ship had a huge contingent of school age children. Enough to start a school, so Jim created one. Everyone with a degree was signed up to help out. If anyone reached the end of their high school years, they were expected to continue and earn a college degree. This served several functions. Jim understood that a community – a society – can very much so either rise up or collapse. He had degreed in history and this was a matter he'd studied extensively. There would be no hillbilly society, nor lazy surfer type atmosphere on board. They would strive and achieve. In a way Jim was even happy that they had been limited in items brought onboard, since it meant no X-boxes or other electronic toys were available that would suck the life out of the children, denying them the drive to accomplishing anything.

He had little argument from the triumvirate. Gordon, an engineer, loved the idea of education, as did the Captain. But Terri fretted about the kids being overworked. And that was the other reason for the school. Idle minds are the devil's workshop. He didn't want people lounging around with nothing to do but gossip. It was a miracle they had made it this far, and would take another to land safely on New Earth. To do that, they had to eliminate dissent. It would be easy for a single disenchanted passenger to open a hatch, and everyone on SS 222 would be dead. With gruesome massacre that had occurred in the dining room, there certainly were unhappy passengers onboard. It was to be a three year trip. Hopefully short enough that if Jim could keep them preoccupied, they might just make it to New Earth happy and healthy.

With XJ2 and XJ4 secured and the XJ1 docking area repaired, the time for departure had arrived. The nuclear engines had not been damaged during the emergency maneuvers to avoid XJ1, and were fully powered, or as close as needed. With everything properly prepared, the ship headed into open space. It would be traveling away from Earth, accelerating all the way, before turning around and heading back toward the Sun. SS 222 would use Jupiter's gravity to assist in the acceleration process while heading as close to the Sun as possible. If everything went as planned, they would cross over into the seventh dimension and the path to New Earth. Easy enough to say. The schedule was for a final touchdown on New Earth in about three years from now. If everything went as planned that is.

This Is Lanny Fillmore

It was supposed to have been a plum job. A rocket off Earth before it melted down. As the son of a powerful Senator, his qualifications for the position were exactly that – son of a powerful Senator. That, and quite frankly, what Lanny suspected was murder. To be more specific, the job he had been given was reserved for what were termed "The Advance Rocket Teams." These were the much smaller rockets launched into space ahead of the space stations with the purpose of preparing and prepping the new planet's landscape for the multitudes of people arriving afterwards. The advertisements billed the rockets as very high tech, and therefore those who earned spots on these craft needed a wide variety of talents. They would have to be part scientist, part ecological expert, part horticulturalist, part meteorologist, and part adventurer. Their missions would be to sail into deep space – often without companionship – to unknown planets, with the necessary equipment to ensure the planet was properly supplied with air, water, or other basic needs for the colony to be created.

The rockets were small, cramped, and short of supplies. In Lanny's case, after a year the reconstituted water tasted slightly of urine and for a three year trip he was stocked with two thousand meals – enough for not quite two meals a day. And that was to cover for his time on the planet as well while waiting for crops to grow, if they would at all. The only extra item Lanny brought was a video game machine and some games.

In their brief but intense training, these young heroes were to be taught how to read maps of the section of space they were to populate, in case any adjustments were needed to the flight path, became experts on basic electrical issues, such as fixing HVAC units, and masters of building, working on, and repairing the computers on board their rocket ships.

Because of the high training requirements, provided in a short amount of time, these openings were only available to the best and brightest of the nation's scientific community. Smart young men and women with lots of knowledge and even more potential. Those earning perfect scores on their SAT's or close to it, only made the first cut. Then there were the physical examinations and psychological testing. After all, how long could someone be alone in such stressful situations without going completely mad? As the intellectual, physical, psychological, and emotional examinations continued, the public were assured... those who selected were the best of the best, and nothing less.

Certainly that wasn't a good description of Lanny Fillmore, who had grown up surrounded by money and whose only trained talent was video games. In no way did he qualify for the available positions requiring young Einsteins, except he had an ace in the whole. Lanny Fillmore was the son of Larry Fillmore. And Larry Fillmore was Senator Fillmore, the powerful head of the Ways and Means committee, privy to every fact regarding the plans to send space stations to far off planets. It was his father, Senator Fillmore, that had reviewed the specifications for the advance rockets. After having his staff provide an analysis of the duties required for the trip, he came to the decision; his youngest son Lanny was perfect for the position. How could that be? How could his lazy and unmotivated son be qualified in any way for such an elevated position? The answer was quite simple. All of the training, the extra studies and preparation, were in case of problems. If anything went wrong, there was someone make it right.

What if nothing went wrong? Then what you had was essentially a three year ride staring at a blank window and doing nothing. As the Senator bitterly but accurately stated, "Lanny's been preparing for this job his whole life." Or as Chief of Staff Jim LaBlanc further analyzed, "You have to be able to run a microwave, maybe duct tape a leaking cooling coil, and relax. The computers do the rest. And if they don't, with the flip of a switch, the backup computers take over."

So on the launch day for the advance rocket ship to New Earth, Lanny was picked up by a private limousine with nothing but the clothes on his back, a video gamer, and a stack of video games. The limousine stopped on the edge of the tarmac – Lanny told to wait in the vehicle. His escorts calmly cut a hole in the security fence and disappeared. A few minutes later Lanny saw them, for only an instant and in the distance, carrying what seemed to be a young boy, about Lanny's size and age. When they appeared again, it was with the young man's space suit in their hands, or so Lanny supposed. He was ordered to put the suit on before being rushed to the rocket ship with specific instructions. No matter what Lanny heard in his ear piece, he was to reply with a crisp, "Check!" That was it. Nothing else. This flight, they explained, had already begun the countdown for takeoff. As long as Lanny stayed on board, he was going into space.

Soon after the final instructions were cleared and the rocket fired up. As Lanny looked around at his surroundings, it was with a sense of confusion. Sure Earth was on the verge of melting down, but did he want this? Hell no! He was a slacker who wanted others to go and figure out what needed to be done. He just wanted to play Death Mark III – Sniper Edition. He hadn't been informed this was planned, even as he came onboard the ship. No goodbye from his mother, and certainly not his father. Making an examination of the small rocket ship's insides, there were two things of value. One was a plug for his game player, and the other a letter. It was from Senator Fillmore, providing nothing more than a laundry list of his supplies, such as where the food could be found and how much was on board, and advice on how to conserve. Within twenty minutes of being launched into outer space, Lanny was relaxing, munching on some chips and playing Medieval Warrior Destroyer. So much for pre flight training.

How was the three year ordeal? Lanny became a five star sniper, saved the Draclions from the evil forces of Lur the Conqueror, and became supreme King of medieval England and France. There were other games, but those were his biggest accomplishments. When the ship reached the seventh dimension, it was… Well, there are no words to describe other dimensions to those who've never been to such heights. It would be no easier than describing green to someone who has been blind since birth. If he could have, Lanny would have stayed in the seventh dimension forever, but as his food was limited and the rocket on autopilot, Lanny was content for the brief time enjoyed there.

Upon reaching Planet ELS 107, or New Earth as it was to be known, the Rocket made several passes around the golden colored orb, the ship's instruments reading and storing information on the New Earth's outer shell before selecting the best location for landing. The two high sierra plateaus were identified; one at ten thousand feet, and the other at five thousand. Lanny was pleasantly pleased when offered the chance to select which of the two would be taken. His first real decision in three years. Choosing the lower plateau he watched as the craft eased into the atmosphere and landed, sending a spray of the golden kernels in it's wake. When Lanny first disembarked, he felt as if entering a huge bowl of Captain Crunch cereal, without the milk of course.

Though he didn't know it, he was the first human being ever to have landed on a foreign planet, walking outside without a protective suit, not that he was that impressed. His first thought in the daytime heat was of the water transformer. Short of food and with water tasting of pee, he couldn't wait to get it running. But at a hundred forty degrees, he barely was able to remove the water transformer from the hold and attach plates containing the catalyst before returning inside to pass out. As he closed the door to the rocket, he could hear the rush of air beginning to flow through the water transformer and the hiss of what he assumed was steam being produced. It shouldn't be long he thought, maybe an hour or so before water would be created.

Mr. Newton, Let Me Introduce You To Mr. Einstein

The key to the seventh dimension had been right there before us for quite some time. All we had to do was look to our greatest scientists and of course their greatest accomplishments. First, Isaac Newton came along with his ground breaking formula of F=ma, followed by Albert Einstein and $E=mc^2$. Both men in their lifetimes shook the scientific community to its very roots with their signature formulas changing the way we view the world. Einstein's theories built upon Newton's and helped explain what was, really wasn't quite that. For example, Newton determined how fast an apple would fall from a tree, while Einstein proved that not only does the apple fall to earth, but the earth rises up to meet it. Who could have imagined such ideas, let alone prove them?

If these men can be compared through their body of work and more specifically their theories, then this is even more true through an analysis of their formulas. Both formulas have a single common element, that being "m" for mass. To marry the two concepts together is quite simple. Using basic math, each formula is solved for m, with the resulting formulas of m=F/a and $m=E/c^2$. Then you can combine the formulas, which can be written as $F/a=E/c^2$.

Up to this point, everything is quite basic. Before we go further a little explanation might help. "F" stands for force, "E" for energy, "a" for acceleration and "c" the speed of light – the fastest speed humans can move in our four dimensions. It is "a" and "c" that are the keys to the seventh dimension. If the formula is adjusted to determine what "c" equals, it would be as follows: c=sqrt(Ea/F).

To reach the seventh dimension, "c" must be greater than speed of light, or 186,282 miles per second. Einstein was very clear on this point, that can't happen, not in our universe… not in the four dimensions. And that is the key. The seventh dimension isn't in our Universe. It is… well, in the seventh dimension. To fool the rules of physics and Einstein, the key is to manipulate "a" or acceleration.

Since "c" equals the speed of light – or the fastest that anything can move – the trick is to find a way to increase one of the elements on the other side of the equation so quickly that the total exceeds "c." And this became possible with the discovery of the "crank" the smallest particle ever, with a mass just this side of a photon. With the use of the crank, a new acceleration almost at the speed of light was possible in the following manner. The space station was to accelerate toward the speed of light. It wouldn't reach that, or even get close, but it didn't have to, although it did have to generate huge speed. As the space station soared through space, a tube wrapped around the space station, no wider than a quarter inch in diameter, would begin shooting "cranks" in both directions through the tube. As they were almost weightless, the cranks would rocket at each other at the speed of light, or just below. When they collided the resulting impact was, when combined with the speed of the space station, a point with an acceleration higher than the speed of light. Once that occurred, SS 222 would be under the laws and guidelines of other dimensions, in this case the seventh dimension.

That was the theory at least. Once in the seventh dimension, everything would work as before, but with three additional dimensions as well, and that was the trick. Utilizing these dimensions would allow the space station to traverse half way across the universe to its new home, and in a very short period of time. How did they know this would work, making a trip of three years for SS 222, while for others it would take decades? It was all in the calculations and seemed very complex. But once one entered the seventh dimension, it all made sense. When you left the seventh dimension, you couldn't go back, not unless you managed the trick again. But just as a blind man can remember the color green from when he could see, you would remember the seventh dimension, and be glad for the experience.

It Be The Pirates Disease Matey!

As Jim LaBlanc stared out the front window of the bridge, it wasn't Newton's or Einstein's theories running through his mind. Whenever he needed quiet time, this was where he came. Other than Captain Majewski and Ensign Beers, who shared the duties of being on the bridge, there was rarely anyone else here. As for the other passengers, few had access. As for Gordon and Terri, they only spent time on the bridge for the triumvirate's regularly scheduled or emergency meetings.

It was here on the bridge where one could be gravity free, the only area of the space station where that was true. While the outside body of the ship had a regular rotation that offered a pseudo gravity due to the living quarters being built on the outer hull of the ship, this spinning would be a problem for the bridge. If the bridge spun along with the rest of the ship, one would get dizzy staring out the four small windows on the front of the craft, to say nothing of the natural spin the room would have. Therefore, the ship was designed with an anti-rotation mechanism on the bridge, allowing it to remain fixed in place no matter how fast the rest of the ship turned.

When he wanted to think, Jim liked coming here. Quiet, he was able to float weightless in the air… very relaxing. Being on the bridge also gave Jim time to tutor Captain Majewski, whom he projected as the leader for the small colony once they landed on New Earth. When they arrived, it would be difficult to have elections among such a small group. And Jim worried, with such a small segment of people onboard, a clever small, but extreme group, could hijack the election and insert themselves into power. As far as he was concerned, if Captain Majewski could be trained, that would bring stability to the colony, something Jim was sure would be needed.

Today his thoughts drifted to the triumvirate… Almost one year in as the space station began its slow turn toward earth before blasting toward the sun, the three headed leadership model was showing cracks. They were initially hailed as great leaders for their swift action in saving the lives of those on board. The decision to save the youngest was considered brilliant. Less discussed but just as strongly believed, keeping the potential despot, Senator Fillmore, from gaining entrance was life saving for many onboard. The goodwill created by these decisions lasted for some time. Food had been served evenly, with the three leaders sharing in their fill of the human food, which was sliced from the bodies and chopped up for consumption. With everyone involved in the school or maintaining the ship, there was little time for discontent.

But problems were beginning to crop up, as Jim expected. He always said that when things were at their best, that only meant bad times were approaching. In the case of SS 222, the problems began with an illness that attacked the passengers. Mysterious bone aches, dental problems, and physical weakness had been reported. But something worse had invaded. There was a laziness infiltrating the ship, Jim felt it himself. That was all it took to start the rumors. Stories of space spirits seeping onboard to take over the minds of the crew. Claims of sightings of wisp like ghosts floating past were increasing, along with the claim that aliens (Martians being the most popular) were infiltrating their ranks, planning for an ultimate takeover.

Jim didn't worry about that. What concerned him more was how the three leaders behaved in this time of trouble. Gordon, a rather grumpy man even in the best of times, took to bitterly complaining that those starting rumors were the real problem. Terri was little better with constant medical leave for one ailment after another. But that was expected of an engineer and an office worker.

The disappointment was Captain Majewski, who reacted not with leadership, but by withdrawing from others. Spending more time on the bridge – with the remainder locked away in his quarters. As the mood of the ship declined, so too did the Captain's disposition. Rather than showing the characteristics of a leader, he seemed happy to behave as the perfect follower.

It had taken some time to determine the source of the problems, and was rather simple once the focus moved away from the rumors of evil spirits. It was the nurse who concluded it was not some sort new age outer space bug. The answer was no different than the scourge of many a ship on the open seas from centuries ago. With the limited meals on board providing only so much of vitamins C and D, the problem was announced as scurvy and rickets, ailments of sailors in centuries past.

That was the good news, the mystery had been solved. The bad news was both ailments would have a severely detrimental effect on the ship's moral, and if unchecked would result in continued deteriorating health, even to the point of death. How does one get vitamins C and D? Fruits and vegetables, something unavailable on SS 222, other than the dwindling supply of frozen meals.

The thin chef had been consulted many times since the diagnosis, hoping for recommendations on how to improve the ship's diet. All were failure. That seemed to be the theme with the thin chef, who it turned out had the metabolism of a flea, as he was caught on several occasions stuffing himself with the pre-made meals. Amazingly his frail body could cram down six or seven meals in a single sitting. When confronted the snide chef, snarling like a cornered rat, said, "You pigs! You want me to eat what? I am graduated from the CIA! I don't eat human! And I don't care if we all die!"

Finally the decision had to be made. The thin chef was fired and locked in food bin 200, the result of sneaking into the food stores to pilfer even more meals. In his place was a man by the name of Jeremy Braun, who's previous food experience had been working in a school cafeteria with a small turn as a butcher's helper.

When the new head chef requested a meeting to share something extraordinary with the triumvirate, there was little excitement. Jeremy who tended to be the dramatic side, instead of simply explaining himself, demanded a private meeting regarding the health epidemic. When Jeremy entered the bridge for the meeting, it was holding what looked like frozen old snake skins and stinking of poop.

"Jeremy! What is this?"

Sounding excited, Jeremy said, "Look! Look inside! It's Ann Gardner's lower colon. See?"

Jim couldn't think of anything he wanted to see less than the bowels of a dead person. But as Jeremy floated forward, he had no choice.

"What? Aw god... I don't see anything but poo."

Jamming the colon under Jim's face, Jeremy said, "See? See? See what's inside?"

Almost passing out from the odor, Jim said weakly, "Please... get that away from me."

"What? Oh, alright. But don't you get it?"

"Yes, we now know what Ann Gardner's last meal was. This isn't a detective show, I don't care. We all know how she died. She was killed. Affixation. Unfortunate but necessary."

"Oh yes you do care!"

"Why?"

"Why? Let's get the gardens going! We've got seeds, lots of them. I don't know what, but all kinds."

Shoving Jeremy away, Jim was beginning to see what precious cargo was contained in Ann Gardner's intestines. "You mean to tell me?"

"Yes! On a hunch I started pulling the intestines apart. We've got them all labeled, just in case we have to... you know. And this is the last thing we'd eat, because, it's full of... well, you know."

"Yes, since the thin chef ate so much. We are short. I have no doubt of that."

Jeremy laughed. "Most definitely. An eating machine. But... now we have... fruit! Or vegetables, or both. Who knows? We've got the seeds anyway."

It was a simple matter. Already the metallic garden troughs were being filled with the waste from the water treatment equipment. The stench was horrific, but there was no other easy location to set the refuse. But now... Should he call a meeting?

Sadly, no. Jim would take control of the matter himself, as it seemed he did with most issues. More and more he missed the administrative and motivational skills of Senator Fillmore. There were many negatives in the Senator's personality, but now he was gone, his talents were certainly missed.

Within a day the gardens were seeded and by the end of the week, the remaining intestines had been plundered for anything that resembled seeds. With plenty of water, the gardens slowly began to take shape as small green sprigs began to sprout from the stench of the troughs.

If only the same could be said of Jim's attempts to instill leadership into the triumvirate. The talk and negative vibes that had begun with stories of ghosts began to spread. It was now clear to Jim – unrest was starting. They wanted elections, something Jim detested. Elections meant verbal combat, aggressive behavior, and worse of all, Jim might lose his job and therefore control. They always get ugly, elections that is. As a sign of the potential problems ahead, the ship had just announced its second pregnancy, unfortunately both were fourteen year old girls. Not the kind of positive stories the current leadership needed in an election cycle.

Who Shall Lead This Nation?

With SS 222 accelerating toward the Sun, leadership of the space ship had changed dramatically. The three headed monster had been deposed in a violent uprising. Captain Majewski had been beat up and was now responsible for little more than steering the space station. Jim was in jail for attempted murder, charged by the new leader, Kevin, who was convinced that Jim and Gordon should be executed for their roles in the failure to allow XJ1 to properly dock with the space station.

How had this occurred? When asked about such large changes in direction over a short period of time, Jim was fond of saying, "Events." Events such as two underage pregnancies, one which ended in the mother's death during child birth, combined with two other deaths, one possibly due to rickets. The other? No one knew. The child complained for days of internal pains, and a last ditch attempt to go in and find the problem was a disaster. Captain Majewski's erratic behavior during this time wasn't of any assistance, as he ensconced himself in his rooms for the critical operation, allowing others to describe what he was thinking and why.

And there were additional charges – food theft – made by none other than the thin chef, his form of revenge toward both the Captain and Jim. Despite many eye witnesses to the thin chef's pilfering habits, he claimed to be too small to have gobbled down so much, something people unaware of the facts were inclined to believe. After all, he couldn't have weighted more than ten pounds over a hundred.

If not for his ability to steer the ship, Captain Majewski would have been locked away in jail beside Jim. That and Ensign Beer's loyalty to the man who had taken him under his wing. Beers had refused to guide the space station alone, insisting Captain Majewski be by his side. Things had gotten so out of control that now not one, but both pregnancies were being blamed on the Captain, despite the now deceased girl's boyfriend claiming fatherhood. The vindictive thin chef had gone so far as to state that Captain Majewski had planned to secretly abort the babies in order to eat them in a private religious ceremony. He claimed this knowledge because Captain Majewski demanded that he skewer the babies and roast them with potatoes taken from the garden.

Jim had heard and seen worse in his time, but not in the limited confines of space. He was confident of being released… that is if a lynch mob didn't come for him first. On the positive side, it brought Captain Majewski out of his funk. Every day he appeared on the bridge, prepared for the day's work. The best Jim could figure was the weight of having the responsibility of killing everyone in dining room A had been too much for the young man to handle. Jim was partially to blame, throwing on the added responsibility of leading their band to New Earth. Yes, that was a lot, more than the Captain Majewski could take.

As for Terri, she showed no concern for Captain Majewski or his plight, focusing on protecting Gordon from the charges of denying XJ1 from boarding. Gordon had taken the stubborn position that yes, he had done so, and would do it again. It was him or those following Senator Fillmore on XJ1. In fact, Gordon loudly stated, had he not acted, the only person currently onboard SS 222 that would be alive today would be Kevin, due to his connection to his wife. To Jim's surprise, Gordon even put out that Kevin's wife might have been sleeping with the Senator, something everyone suspected, but of course there was no proof. This behavior was so out of normal for Gordon, to make unfounded accusations, but showed the passions flowing about the space ship.

As tempers flared, events were not playing out in a court room as would happen on Earth, but rather through insults hurled across the dining room by packs of people leaning more toward gangs than groups separated based on opinion. The triumvirate had in a moment gone from heroes to cannibals, with Kevin and his supporters claiming that hidden somewhere additional food was on board XJ1, for surely the Senator wouldn't have arrived on SS 222 without excess provisions. Further, the sole reason for the refusal of the entry of XJ1 to the space station was personal power, and that the triumvirate – in league with Jim – were more than happy to snack on the bodies of others in exchange for obtaining power.

In assessing Kevin, and his chief aide, Barry, Jim had little interest in either. Thick headed brutes he described as "Charging Rhinos." Once they chose a direction, they couldn't be swayed from it no matter the facts or situation. Jim was now cast as the dark lord, whispering in the ear of the three former leaders. In a way Jim thought that true. Yes, very much so. The difference was he wasn't advising as accused, muttering in private of treason, cannibalism, and conglomerating power, but rather of leadership and how to manage their small group.

Jim considered the current disagreements and arguments as a form primaries and debates. Each side putting forth their ideas in an attempt to garner a majority. If that was the case, then Jim and his three headed leader were holding the cards. To be sure they had been greedy in some of their decisions, but then who wouldn't be in their situation? Show him one person who would have given over their seat to someone else. They all in a way had that option before getting in the rockets that left Earth. It was only the greedy that were on the space station. In sum and total, Jim and the triumvirate had acted for the good of all. Could the same now be said of Kevin and Barry?

No. Kevin was exposing himself as a wining simpleton who gained followers as much by complaining as anything else. There were no agenda or solutions to the current problems, nor any vision for what to do once landed on New Earth. His saving grace was that he was quick enough to determine that Jim and Gordon had stopped XJ1 from docking, and loud enough in pointing out such deviousness that everyone else heard.

Jim was convinced that just as events had overtaken them, tossing them from the leadership positions, new events would bring freedom and provide vindication. The gardens were producing vegetables and even some small amounts of fruit. With that, the health and mood of the entire passenger list was improving. Not much mind you, but enough that Jim made sure Terri explained to everyone in earshot that it was the three who had started the gardens not Kevin or the brutish Barry. Why there was even a rumor the thin chef had been spotted stealing tomatoes.

Yes, events were happening, as another child had become deathly ill. This one apparently had a history of sickness, but that didn't stop Jim from recommending to Terri that she demand Kevin save the life of the child, no different from the demands Kevin put upon Captain Majewski. When Terri objected to the tactic, Jim pointed out the best way to save her husband was to remove the current leadership. As Jim well knew, politics can become very ugly. And so Terri reluctantly became the ship's unofficial town crier, shouting out her sides positions. Already Jim could hear stories of how some of those who had been most vocal in the removal of the three were now stating their objections to Kevin and Barry.

Barry. He was the wild card, or one of two wild cards.
Better still, the violent wild card. It was Barry that had put the
beating on Captain Majewski in the uprising, allowing Kevin
to ascend into the leadership position. He had since provided
two more examples of his ability to distribute extreme
violence and was now feared… and becoming hated. Were
Barry able to replace Kevin as leader and form some sort of
inner circle, then all was lost, or so Jim thought. But so far,
Barry seemed what Jim had always suspected. A lout. A big,
violent thug. Brutish in behavior and crude in thought. Still
he had to be watched. If he were to advance past his thuggish
personality, he could become quite the enemy. And if placed
in a nascent society, planted in a new planet… such are the
stories brutal tyrants are made of.

Then there was the other wild card, Dolly Fillmore.
She had remained aloof of all the turmile. The battles, the
personalities, the insults. She had thrown her lot in neither
with Kevin nor the three. Had she supported Kevin, he would
have been harder to fend off, and all four of the former leaders
might be in jail now. Conversely, with a few choice words,
she might have been able to avert Kevin's takeover. But she
did neither, choosing a much more circumscript path,
allowing events to play out as she waited on the sidelines for
one side or the other to prove themselves superior.

As Jim waited in prison, he seemed rather content regarding events… the future ones to come that is. A trial had been scheduled, the charges being Jim had intentionally delayed, then stopped XJ1 from docking with SS 222. Further he did so with the full knowledge this meant the likely death of all on board XJ1. If that was all, Jim was confident of victory. He would, like Gordon before him, admit to the charge, stating his refusal to allow Senator Fillmore to board was done in the best interest of those already on SS 222. After all a jury of his peers would include only those saved by his their decision. And he had one more trick up his sleeve. Once the jury was selected, the passenger list would be leaked. Not the original, but the one containing the names of those Senator Fillmore requested be segregated from the others so that they might be sent back to Earth. And Jim would make sure that as many jurors as possible would find their names on that list.

Yes… events. They twisted and turned in ways never imagined. But if one was clever, those events could be manipulated to happen just when they were most fortuitous to certain people. The battle for leadership of the people of New Earth wasn't over. In fact it had barely begun, and they hadn't even landed. Hell, they hadn't even reached the seventh dimension. Jim, through previous events, had already thrown in his lot. He was loyal to the three, certainly not Kevin and Barry. That gave the three the experience and talent of Jim. How well were things going? Today he received a tomato for desert. His first since on board SS 222. Biting into it, he smiled. It was sweet with just the slightest bit of tang… in short it tasted of victory.

Trial… In The Seventh Dimension

The trial was to be presided over by Angel Heatherborne, the lawyer who earned passage on SS 222 through the luck of having a newborn. He was a bit of an unknown to Jim, one of the many who passed through the offices of Congressmen and Senators with dreams of success. And what was success? All kinds Jim had learned. Some hoped one day to be President while others just wanted to make a few bucks. Sure, there were those determined to make a difference... more than you would expect. But ultimately, most drifted away... to other jobs, careers, and ways of life.

The trial was expected to take a day or so... maybe less. Jim was confident in representing himself while Kevin, who took Jim's decision as a challenge to his authority, declared that he personally would present what he described as, "The state's case." What state he was referring to, neither Jim nor Angel were sure of, considering they were millions of miles from Earth and no one had been elected to anything, state or otherwise. Kevin's dramatics were largely ignored. After all, much more was at stake than Jim's life, which didn't seem to be in very much danger.

In fact the trial was by now considered an afterthought by many if not most of the adults onboard SS 222. Food, in the form of vegetables as well as the promise of fruit in the near future, had vastly changed the ship's health and mood. Thanks to Jim and Terri spreading the word, the goodwill earned for such a success had been credited to what was now referred to as the "Party of Three," and not Kevin and Barry, who created an opposition party. That being "The Fillmore," in honor of the Senator denied of a space on SS 222. Further, Jim's trick of releasing the list of the names of those who were to be deported from the space station had been a wild success. Hard to convict someone for saving your life.

It seems that now everyone had someone to compare the Captain's poor leadership to – that being Kevin – Captain Majewski didn't seem so evil, incompetent, and greedy. Jim knew very well it is easier to complain about others failures than actually make things happen. That was Kevin's problem right now. He simply didn't have the qualities a leader is made of. This in turn led to another question. Who would lead the small group of people on SS 222? The final decision regarding elections was that they would take place, but not until the space station had safely landed on New Earth. The decision was based on two main points. It gave both parties time to put together platforms and formally present their case, and if they burned up in the Sun… who really cared?

Jim was pushing hard for Captain Majewski, who had returned somewhat to a more normal behavior. He had even held a private chat with him, apologizing for having thrust him into the leadership position too soon and the two reached an accord. Why not Gordon, or Terri? This recent spate of unpleasant words had pushed Gordon to his limit, and he had taken the insults personally, all of them. That was something a leader in politics just couldn't do. And Terri? Jim would have taken her in a heartbeat, but she was still in the mode of protecting Gordon and didn't want to be taken off task. She preferred to fight for what was right while standing beside her man. That and she quite frankly didn't have the personality for what lay ahead. Defending her husband was one thing, but could she do and say as Jim had seen Senator Fillmore behave? No, that was not possible. Sometimes doing the right thing isn't the easy thing, or even the nice thing. Terri just wasn't that kind of girl.

Immediately Kevin recognized the difficulty he faced in an election. Jim was a master of such events, and the improvement in everyone's diet was rightly or wrongly being credited to Captain Majewski. As one potential voter said, "I don't care if it was Jim or the Captain, what I know is they got it done. I'm healthy, the kids are healthy. What more can I ask for?

Realizing mistakes were made, Kevin decided to take on a role similar to Jim, the power behind the throne. And in doing so, he floated the idea of Manson heading up the ticket. It was a disaster. First of all, this exposed who had revealed to Kevin the betrayal of XJ1, something that upset Manson greatly. He had offered the information in confidence, hoping to give closure to Kevin for the loss of his wife. Manson simply couldn't bear to carry the secret alone. Second, Manson was a fixit guy, a go to guy. He made things happen behind the scenes. But what he wasn't was the head man, the front man. Even the thought terrified him. And finally, even in such a small set of people, could you have a worse last name if running for office than Manson?

Finally it was decided, Kevin would head the Fillmore party's banner, if for no other reason than the embarrassment of not fielding a candidate. That, and the deep seeded hatred Kevin was beginning to feel toward the Party of Three. It wasn't that he loved and missed his wife. In truth, he didn't. There's had been a marriage of convenience. Kevin was handsome and came from a well respected family and his wife a hard charging, smart work-a-holic. After marriage, Kevin was prepared to ease into a life of staying out of his wife's way as she ruthlessly advanced her career. She would have the position, earn the money, and build the nest egg. Kevin had earned a fairly simple sales position with low quotas and lots of time for golf, frequent trips, and plenty of opportunities to shag chicks on the side. But now? His wife was dead, he was broke, and there were no girls to shag. His life was a misery.

And who was to blame? Certainly not Kevin, who never pointed a finger at himself. He was the kind that could always fine someone else to blame for his failures. And Captain Majewski was the perfect foil. Thin almost to the point of being scrawny, not the kind who dressed very well, with a direct, almost confrontational way of presenting himself, that left much to be desired. It was easy for the smooth talking Kevin with his impeccable presentation skills to see the Captain as the source of his problems.

The trial was a necessity, even though Kevin knew the battle was lost. He had determined to keep Barry on his side regardless the outcome. Who knew how life on New Earth would be. It never hurt to have a huge violent man as a best friend, especially when one has the talent Kevin was in possession of – for making enemies. And Barry was almost psychopathic in his desire to try Jim. He seemed to carry some sort hatred for the Party of Three. Maybe it went back to his time in dining room A when they had issues. Maybe even before. Or maybe Barry was just a hateful kind of a guy, all the more reason to stay on his good side.

If the timetables were to be trusted, the space station would make the last accelerated dive toward the Sun a few days after the trial. This plunge toward the sun had two options; death or the seventh dimension. If it was death, Kevin might as well keep his mind off his impending doom by taking one last stab at making his enemies' lives miserable. If they succeeded and made it to the seventh dimension, shortly afterwards it would be a resounding victory for the Party of Three. Jim had already secured forty of the fifty or so votes that would be cast. In fact he was so confident of victory he was considering of voting for Kevin himself. No one had to know, and they would have to make friends with The Fillmore party after the election. Jim understood, that's how things worked in elected politics. Your enemy today was part of tomorrow's coalition. At least if you wanted to be successful in the long run.

Even as the day progressed and the trial headed toward its bland but ultimate ruling of innocent, Jim couldn't help but be nervous. He had used all of his political gamesmanship tricks and talents to take his mind off the obvious, that he might soon be fried like an egg. As people cheered and shook his hand – the case of "The State" vs. LaBlanc coming to a successful close – Jim barely had a smile on his face. He didn't want to die, but his internal pessimisms had convinced him of that. Instead of joining his supporters in a small celebration, he chose instead to hunt down his wife Helga. Make that ex-wife. She had been shocked by his behavior on that first day on SS 222, and lost all confidence in him, condemning his part in what had been done in dining room A. Her last words to him were, "No Jim! I can't. I von't. I believe in you... you can do anytink. But now? You feed us humans so that vee can live more. No. I'm done vit you."

Seeing her former husband approach, Olga spun away. Once the aura of your loving husband is gone, it never returns, especially when replaced with the image of a serial cannibal killer who turned everyone else either into one of those beasts or the food they ate. He was a god to her once, but now? More devil than saint... and of no use.

Jim stopped a good distance away, his eyes still focused on the love of his life. He had done the right thing, saved lives, possibly stopped a monster from becoming their leader. But Helga... she was so emotional and care free. That was always something he needed more of to balance his otherwise calculated life. But she was also easily swayed by whatever was in front of her at the moment and sometimes... problems needed more thought than Helga was willing to apply. Would he have set everyone free so that Helga would speak to him? No. Just because she wasn't interested in or willing to put forth the effort to consider their situation, and how to get out of it, didn't mean he should sacrifice everyone's lives for her delicate emotional sensitivity.

Land Ho!

Lanny was busy on the edge of his small oasis, carefully stacking the small golden kernels that rimmed his valley. It was slow going since each small sparkling shard was overloaded with all sorts of edges and points on them. When examined closely, they were a cross between oversized pieces of popcorn and tiny scoops of ice cream, with an array of tiny jagged lightening bolts on the outside. They looked and felt like a metal – a very malleable one – say gold. But as he had experienced many times, adding water to the golden kernels exposed them to be anything but, as the sharp edges melted away and the nugget turned to mush.

His camp was located on what he dubbed the low sierra plateau, a few miles from the tall sheer face ridge that separated the low sierra ridge from the high sierra and between two breaks in the ridge where the rock had crumbled, tumbling down to create a manageable slope between the two massive flatlands.

Initially he had hoped to use those gentler inclines to venture about, but quickly the plan was abandoned. Between the razor sharp golden kernels, and the high heat and low cold, Lanny never ventured far from his rocket ship. And with the rocket ship stuffed with dirt and plants, flying about was not such a good option either. The pond had grown to a hundred feet across, surrounded by a lip of mushy dirt a few feet tall. There were three gaps in the rim, the largest flowing out in the direction Lanny considered due east, since that was where the Sun rose in the morning. The other two deposited a small amount of water north and south. To the north and south, there were several hundred miles of empty flat land, caked with golden kernels. To the west was the ridge, and to his east, a hundred miles or possibly two of flat land until it opened up to another ridge that descending into a huge basin. Every day he walked in the main river that headed east, guessing it had moved several miles from him by now, if not further.

It was amazing to him the effect water had on the immediate surrounding area. During the day, the temperature was still well into the hundreds but if he became too hot, Lanny simply splashed on some water to cool off. But if he took even one step off away from the river, the full heat of the day could be experienced. It was as if stepping into a blasting furnace with the heat radiating deep within his skin. At night, the lake was no longer froze all the way, and Lanny felt that was important, allowing water to hold some temperature and flush down river. Though he never stayed to find out, he assumed the river – a yard or so wide – eventually iced over every night, at least where no grass was showing. To his pleasure, the grass was slowly finding its way down the river, and even a tomato plant had managed to survive, though not very well. The ground it seems, once infused with water, was extremely fertile.

Once a week or so Lanny tried to reach the river's end, and it was always the same. At the edge, water poured into the bed of golden kernels, steam billowing off, rising into the air before dissipating into nothing. Beyond the river's end, it was always the same. A shining golden sea of nothing cropped with a bright blue sky. He kept expecting the water in the river to stop its advance, evaporating into the hot air. But as it was explained to him in the envelope received at the beginning of the trip, the planet's air was pumped full of oxygen and hydrogen. So much so Lanny guessed, it didn't seem to want water from the ground.

On the north and south ends of the lake, Lanny had punched small holes in the wall so water could seep into the surrounding land. It had worked, as on both sides of the lake, grass and vegetables were growing, and even a few tiny beginnings of fruit trees. This brought another surprise. As the trees grew, Lanny assumed that if not covered, they would burn in the day and freeze at night. Instead, a protective layer of grass had grown around them, rising up to insulate the trees from the weather. Lanny could only assume the tree's growth was due to the extreme nutrients in the ground overcoming the wide swings in temperature.

His days were now spent cloistered on his oasis; cultivating, spreading, and protecting. It amazed him that he, a spoiled child of privilege with no experience in growing anything had been able to carve out this small piece of Eden on a planet that in many ways was as close to hell as possible.

The first time SS 222 circled the planet, Lanny hadn't spotted nor heard anything. It was the same with the second. But on the third pass, when the reverse thrusters were deployed as the space station crashed toward the ground, Lanny easily picked out the red rockets strapped to the sides of SS 222, as well as the huge white parachutes that pulled against the massive ship's descent. When it crashed, he didn't hear anything, but guessed it was… say ten miles from him – due east. For almost a minute he jumped and whooped for joy. After all, how many years was it since he had seen another human? He calmed quickly enough. One never overexerted ones self in the heat of the day. So slowly, methodically, he returned to his rocket ship and putting on his heaviest most protective clothing and began the trek down the river.

As expected, his thin ribbon of river ended long before arriving at the craft. But he could see a halo of dust surrounding the landing area. What to do? It was getting toward darkness and he didn't want to be exposed when the river froze over. Tomorrow would be soon enough. As he slopped through the quickly chilling water, there was a sense of excitement within him. How long had it been since he'd had a conversation with someone? For some time now he was convinced. Never again would he ever see anyone. He had survived, and now? One never complains when on the verge of being saved. Try as he might, there was no sleep that night. Calm down, calm down. How would he make it over to them? That was a problem. But he was so close, now was not the time to do anything foolish that would jeopardize his life. After all, every day, his river brought him that much closer.

Lanny pondered using the rocket, but the air vents were still jammed with dirt and roots. It would take days to clean them properly. He didn't want to turn up the turbine engines only to damage them. Any long term damage to the ship was unacceptable. It was needed to keep the inside of the rocket ship comfortable. Without it, he would be at the mercy of the elements. Something he had no choice on. That had to be avoided.

Using the rocket ship was still a possibility, but there were other avenues to try first. Staring into the distance where other humans might have landed, Lanny smiled. Home... he was home. For the first time on this strange planet overstuffed with a layer of sharp popcorn like kernels and ridiculous temperature swings, it felt that way. He was home.

Exploring The Possibilities

The first night on New Earth, did anyone sleep? Doubtful, as the passengers took turns staring out the small windows dotted about the ship, the conversations invariably focused on the small pebble like grains that could be seen everywhere. What were they? Were he able to, Jim would have called for the election immediately, as Captain Majewski had made an excellent landing, gliding into what looked like a pillow of golden dust, before slamming into the ground with a loud "Duff!!!" spaying yellow arcs of dirt that shined in the late evening sun. Instead he was regulated to staying in the bridge with the other members of the Party of Three; Captain Majewski, Gordon, and Terri. Joining them was Ensign Beers who, along with the Captain, was busy reading the results of the air sample for the outside.

It was silly in a way. There was only one spacesuit – a leaky one at that – for the entire ship. It wasn't likely they would live in such hibernation forever, or even very long. But in the minds of the passengers of SS 222, who had been raised on the horrors of countless movies exposing the dangers of alien planets, simply venturing into the night was considered foolhardy. With this in mind, the three headed leadership ignored the preliminary test results that were clear in their conclusions – the air was fine. Instead they summoned the space suit as if it were a religious oracle, debating who would be the first outside. It was clear Captain Majewski wanted the honor, scratching a leg nervously and darting his eyes about, but for some reason he refused to put his name forward. Finally Terri, a grin on her face said, "Yes Brian. You should be the one. You've earned it."

With all the excitement of a kid at Christmas, the Captain pulled on the suit and waited until morning when temperatures were supposed to improve from the current negative forty degrees. With the first rays of the Sun, he stepped nervously to the docking station door and waited. First, he sealed the docking room from the rest of the ship, and then opened the door to the outside. Before stepping out, he said in his most serious voice, as if being recorded, "With this step… mankind has arrived, and will survive."

With each foot put forward, he felt the "Pop! Pop! Pop!" as the sharp gold colored ingots sliced into the rubber bottom of the spacesuit's boots. Reaching down to pick up one of the golden rocks, Captain Majewski said, "Ow! Oh no, it pierced the suit!" Turning to return inside, he slipped and fell on the loose gravelly surface, ripping the pants. Standing up to see the disaster, he began to run back to the docking area, but as he did so, he slowed down – then stopped, taking in a deep breath of air.

A voice shouted, "He's breathing! He can breathe the air! Come on!"

There was a push forward, no different than fans fighting for good seats at a rock concert or entering a theme park, the rush to get outside overtaking caution. The doors were thrown open, and the passengers of SS 222 took their first breaths of fresh air since, well even before leaving earth. This was quickly followed by screams of pain and a hurried retreat back to the ship, the bottoms of their feet cut and sliced by the sharp yellow rocks.

Despite the injuries, laughter and jokes abounded. They had made it. It had sounded impossible, but they were here, and there was air to breathe. While injured feet were bandaged, voices babbled excitedly before the call came for Captain Majewski. What was next?

Next? Well… he didn't know. With all the work needed to properly navigate through the seventh dimension and land safely on New Earth, what had to be done next hadn't occurred to him. This was the largest ship ever to land on a foreign land, or so he imagined. He had hoped to do so with minimal damage and deaths. No landing gear, short two rockets. In the confusion and excitement of landing, he had forgot that there might be something to do after that. His mind was literally a blank, forcing him to say, "Um… Can I go see?"

With all the conflict he'd faced during the trip to New Earth, he expected to be ridiculed, insulted, and shouted down. Possibly even jailed. Instead he was presented with a sea of happy faces and a friendly, "Sure, take your time."

Despite the wide variety of missing provisions on board SS 222, the post landing instructions had been delivered intact – a thin packet of papers including some drawings and brief instructions. Reading the contents brought on a wave of depression, directing the Captain to retrieve two industrial sized water transformers. He knew instantly there was no such equipment on board. Yet another necessity left behind on Earth. But just like the dad working late at night to assemble the children's toys before Christmas, the Captain had scanned the instructions without making a proper read. And just like the lazy dad, when the Captain read again – further down – the instructions explained the water transformers could be found in the aft of the ship, but could only be accessed from the outside.

Quickly a search party was organized, but before they could depart, three pairs of metallic sandals were fashioned so Captain Majewski could lead Barry and Manson to the back of the ship. Sure enough, there were two large sealed storage bins as described. Opening one revealed two spigots similar to the one Lanny was operating, only with a tap diameter of four feet instead of two. Placing them firmly on a bed of golden nuggets near the middle of the ship, the catalyst slats were inserted, and soon a rush of wind flowed through the large tap with loud whooshing sounds as they returned inside, the temperatures outside passing one hundred degrees and quickly rising.

Sharing the metallic sandals, people began to roam in and out of the ship to examine the water transformers or wander about. With so many people entering and leaving in such harsh weather, it quickly became apparent rules had to be made. Already the air conditioning units on SS 222 were working overtime to keep up with the hot air blowing in from outside and a decision had to be made – when could people leave SS 222 and for how long? With the first attempt to bring order to the milling crowds, Kevin objected, pointing out an elected government had not been obtained yet. This was exactly the opportunity Jim was looking for. Calling everyone to the dining room, quickly a quorum was obtained, followed by a vote. Within an hour, Captain Majewski had been chosen to lead their small group. This time by an overwhelming majority.

Assuming his new duties, the Captain made his first decrees. A curfew was issued, stating for now there were for now only two allowed times for going outside. Early morning and at dusk. The second was a recommendation of a formal physical regimen for all on board. The gravity of the space ship in space had been far weaker than New Earth, and had left the passengers weak compared to current conditions. The Captain knew hard work was coming and lots of it. For that, healthy workers were needed. For those who wanted to go outside, schedules were drawn up.

Finally, the garden staff, which had done such a wonderful job of growing fruits and vegetables while in space, were commissioned to collect samples of the golden nuggets and begin experimentation on them. That is after they reconstructed the gardens, most of which were damaged in the rough landing and overturned when the cylindrical like ship came under the gravitational pull of New Earth, dumping plants, fruit trees, and dirt everywhere. Otherwise landing had been fairly damage free.

The golden nuggets. What were they, and were they of any use? The instructions only made vague references of the planet's air being packed with oxygen and hydrogen and that the soil was similarly constructed, and might be good for growing crops. Instead, it looked as if they had landed in the middle of a sea of metal shavings. Hardly the kind of land normally productive for farming.

As Captain Majewski went through his first proclamations, Jim searched for signs of the emotional malaise that had gripped the Captain so tightly during his first tour as leader. Though no concerns showed themselves, that didn't mean they weren't there. He'd seen similar behavior with Senator Fillmore. The stresses of the position could be tearing the Senator to pieces inside without even the slightest outward hints. Of course the Senator always maintained massive quantities of alcohol within his body that masked any ticks or quirks. In fact, Jim was sure that was one reason the Senator so often maintained an inebriated state of mind. Some drunks are easy to figure out. But Senator Fillmore was different. When drunk, there was no seeing past the heavily lidded eyes to peek at the Senator's real intension.

If Captain Majewski was having difficulties, Jim wanted to cut them off at first sign. Whatever it took. A delegation of duties, a delay in the decision making process, even a brief stepping down of responsibilities. He didn't want a repeat of what had happened on board and in space when the Captain had emotionally cracked.

Jim had completed an assessment of the adults on board, and the results were obvious. No one else contained the collection of talents held within Captain Brian Majewski. Hard times were ahead, that was definite. And if they could avoid what Jim was sure would be the disastrous leadership of Kevin, it could be the difference between a hellish existence and the creation of a new free society. Jim didn't kid himself, there were no Utopias. Not on Earth, nor on New Earth. But he preferred to work toward Eden, especially since he'd seen so many times the misery created when good cultures fell into the abyss. It didn't take much effort or a great amount of time for a society to fall. All it took was complacence and laziness… the easiest of atmospheres to foster.

Who Comes Yonder?

What was this planet? It was never a question of where, because that didn't matter. Anywhere in the Universe is about as good as any other. It really comes down to the planet… and the solar system. Well, first the solar system, and then the planet. If the solar system is inhospitable, then so is the planet. A Sun too large, bright, or close means death. With regards to the solar system in the case of Planet ELS 107, or New Earth as it was known, there were no such problems or concerns. In terms of length of day, distance from the Sun, and total planet mass, and a wide variety of other measurements including a moon, New Earth was about as close to the old Earth as one could imagine.

Once the solar system is considered acceptable, the focus turns to the planet. That in turn asks the question of what was on New Earth? The easy answer was a never ending bed of metallic like, razor sharp, and curled up shavings – golden in color. To be a bit more nuanced and clever, you could add extreme heat and cold, because as anyone who had been in the elements – other than dawn or sunset – could verify, the heat and cold were so prominent and profound, that you could almost feel, taste, and touch them when outside. As for the areas beyond the plot of land where the space station had landed, it didn't seem much different. The golden kernels were everywhere, dumped on the ground as if by some sort of celestial grounds keepers who had an obsession with covering the land with them.

When the ground immediately around the space station was dug at and pushed around, only more of the golden nuggets were found. A sample was taken, the nuggets displaying all aspects of metal shavings in look, touch, and feel, covered with an endless matrix of small jagged barbs. When banged upon, they had the dexterity of a metal slightly stronger than gold and were very malleable, causing the nickname, "Almost Gold." Without microscopes or other technically advanced equipment to delve deeper into the kernels, there was no way to investigate to the molecular level, nor determine the elements that made up the golden shards. The best available data was a White Paper written by the original discoverers of the planet. They guessed that the air outside was packed with hydrogen, nitrogen, oxygen and a mix of other elements. But due to the unique magnetic structure of the planet and slight electrical charge within the air, the oxygen and hydrogen were kept from merging, forming into water. This was where the water transformers came into being. With the proper catalyst material attached inside, these machines – which had no moving parts – would utilize the electric charge in the air to fuse hydrogen and oxygen molecules together to create water.

As for the golden kernels, the White Paper suggested they included a wealth of nutrients perfect – once merged with water – for growing plants and trees. As for metals on the planet, there were none, nor were there any within the golden nuggets. The report put forward the position that any metals would have to be mined or otherwise created. These conclusions were hard to accept considering the nuggets brought inside seemed in all respects to be metallic in origin.

That all changed when a glass of water was poured on them and the most amazing conversion occurred. Steam poured off the nuggets, the remaining substance – after bubbling a bit – left behind a gooey and pasty mud. A globular paste that had no resemblance to metal. Several buckets of the kernels were tossed into an empty garden bin and doused with water. After steam bellowed off the heap, the muck remaining behind was seeded with vegetables.

So what was the next step? Between the extreme temperatures and the endless bed of sharp golden kernels surrounding them, there wasn't much other than to wait. A small amount of water was dumped outside the doors of the space station to make a more comfortable walking area for those who chose to spend time outside. Otherwise, the space station had taken on large quantities of water for the trip to New Earth, but compared to the size of the planet, the combined capacity of these water tanks were a drop in a bucket. Captain Majewski made the quick decision to hold back on all testing with the nuggets and water until a better assessment of its ability to grow food was determined.

The first week on the new planet quickly changed from excitement and adventure to watching and waiting… the water transformer that is. Endless hours spent as a superficial wind howled into the tall, wide bowl in the back of the contraption and out the tap in the front. Again a kind of nervous depression fell over the community as it began to feel as if they had landed on a large blanket of sharp metal pebbles surrounded by inhospitable temperatures. Talk was beginning to start of being reduced to staying inside the space station forever.

That all changed when with great excitement one morning when Captain Majewski was awoken to the words, "Water! I think it's water."

A quick inspection of the water transformer showed some sort of moister in small droplets had formed on the rim of the tap blasting out hot air. He wanted to put his hand to it, but as the temperatures were already rising, the Captain chose instead to wipe a rag on the lip before carefully dabbing his tongue on the rag. It seemed to be water, or tasted like it. Well, since water has no taste… could be vodka for all he know, the only other liquid he was aware of that had no taste or odor. But he doubted he'd flown halfway across the Universe to discover a new brand of vodka. With no other options of testing the drops he said hesitantly, "Yes. Think it's water. Good job. Let me know if the situation changes."

That evening he was again roused to be shown some sort of dripping coming from the tap. Going to inspect, this time with a host of curious onlookers, he walked more bravely to the tap. As it was becoming cold outside, he held a hand out under the spray and then licked his hand. "Yup. Water I believe."

Those simple words spread through the space station like wildfire. And with it hope began returning to the small community. They had water, or maybe so. With water, the nuggets could be converted to land, and that combined with seeds meant… yes, they had hope.

All evening and into the night crowds stared in fascination as the water misted, dribbled, and slopped onto the ground, before disappearing into the muddy layer of golden kernels on the ground, steam wisping away as the surrounding kernels slowly turned to paste. When morning came with a stream of water steadily dropping to the mushy ground everyone had to go out, cup a hand, and taste the planet's homemade water.

"We're home now!" announced one of the happy drinkers after a few sips. All day and into the next as the water kept accumulating, the colony's spirits rose, as periodically children went to dance in the mud puddle and then later to slip and slide on the world's smallest ice rink, no more than a few feet wide. Finally Captain Majewski ordered guards on the water transformer while others were outside, one on each side. Not that there was any security or health risk. Rather the orders were given at Jim's recommendation after one of the children accidently bumped into the water transformer.

"Water is going to become very important," said Jim, "We need to start teaching everyone right now. That, and the fact that giving out guard assignments will keep people occupied... let them feel they are part of the process, create a community. Then as the water flow grows, so too will people's confidence in our ability to lead." After a pause to consider his words, Jim added, "But not Barry... no, not Barry at all. He is too... well, you know. Too violent."

The next day, the flow of water became so steady it reached the ground without any breaks, and the second water transformer began to drip. This on top of the announcement that from the mush in the garden bin, seeds had sprouted... everyone was becoming ecstatic.

Caught up in the good mood, Captain Majewski commissioned a small detail to make a path several miles due west. When landing the ship, the computer indicated two small areas that might have water... maybe even plant life. One was hundreds of miles away in the high sierra, but the other might be within walking distance, depending upon how harsh the weather was. When Captain Majewski stared off into the distance, he wondered if he couldn't see just the faintest wisp of steam rising in the air. That or he was imagining things. Either way, he approved four members to make the trek. Gordon would lead in the name of the now official Party of Three, along with the resourceful Manson. The brutish Barry was also assigned, to show party balance. His selection was made after Kevin quickly refused an offer to go along, stating, "I ain't dying for anyone." The last member was Hap Hanson, one of those who had escaped the death of staying in dining room A when Helga kept the door open. Hap was an avid runner and a fitness freak who had shown a desire to be more than just part of their small community.

With orders to return at the first sign of trouble, they were gone at dusk and returned three hours later. While Barry and Hap argued to push forward, Gordon had called off the expedition when in addition to the cold temperatures, a wind started to whip through them, with occasional pieces of the golden nuggets taking to the air. The ensuing argument was nasty, but when Captain Majewski saw their half frozen bodies, he said only, "You can kill yourself another day. Right now we need everyone alive."

"Kill me if you wish. I'm already dead," muttered Barry, glaring bitterly at Gordon.

The Captain was right, or so Jim advised. A failed mission was not good. Bringing back the dead, or dead and never to return? A disaster, and they'd already seen the downside of such events. "Events," Jim reminded the Captain with a smile, "They can make a man or crush him. Now is not the time to find out which." And it wasn't as if the mission was a failure. They claimed to have seen a light in the distance. There were easier ways to follow up on information than losing four men in the cold.

I Bring You Water

The space station, four hundred feet long and eighty feet in diameter, had plowed as much as ten feet into the gravelly ground of golden kernels. That left seventy feet above ground to the top of the space station. Scrambling atop the craft, Captain Majewski earned a good view in all directions. He could see North and South until, in the dim light of the night, there was no more, and to the East was the same. Finally, he turned his attention to the West… there it was. A light. Not a star or otherwise celestial, but rather some sort of man made lighting. That was the Captain's opinion.

There were supposed to be two other spaceships landing on New Earth. Could the light only miles from SS 222 be one of them? Either SS 221 or Advance Ship 25? With no light to provide a better view and the biting cold seeping into his bones, the Captain descended. Convening with the expedition crew and Terri, he said, "Yes, a light. How do you propose we move forward?"

"Simple," offered up Hap, "We go there."

The Captain frowned. The ground was a hazard and the weather unsafe. One mistake could cause death. Already their small colony had lost five people to various deaths. They had been somewhat replaced with three births and a pregnancy. If the colony was to not only survive, but thrive, the good of the community had to be considered. Captain Majewski was convinced Hap would gladly lead the other three to their death without ever considering turning back. He seemed to have made his excellent health a source of pride. What of making a path, dumping water on the golden kernels?

No, too slow. It would take weeks or months. What of making a fast, furious charge? How long was the time between the first crack of dawn and when the heat of the day became oppressive? An hour, if that. The conversation was tabled after more solutions, most similar to the original, were offered. Many would require water, and until it was determined how much water was available, no decision could be made. For the moment, the amount of water available was an ever changing and increasing target. It seemed the water transformers increased production mostly in the morning and evening when the temperatures changed. Therefore, no decision would be made until dawn and the amount of water for the day could be determined.

With morning came good news, Spigot #1 – the first to create water – was now churning out water at a pace similar to a kitchen sink. Possibly several gallons per minute. As for Spigot #2, it was now spitting out small intermittent streams to the ground. With the water around Spigot #1 now pooling and beginning to drain to the east Captain made a simple calculation. Two gallons a minute… more than a hundred gallons an hour. That calculated to, assuming New Earth's day was similar to Earth, roughly twenty five hundred gallons a day, or a quarter of an ordinary home swimming pool. Considering that SS 222 had enough water to take care of the colony, the decision was simple. Using the few containers that were available, the rest of the day was spent tossing water on the golden kernels to make a path to the west. Not wide or deep, just enough to turn the surface kernels from jagged rocks to smooth paste. The entire community was used for the exercise and soon two paths were created, one to take the water containers into the heat and a second to return back. In the heat, peaking at times up to one hundred seventy, everyone was required to take breaks. As the sun began to disappear and temperatures quickly dropped, heading toward zero, the work day was ended, to Hap's loud protests. It was a frustrating but correct decision. Everyone was exhausted and the path no more than an eighth of a mile. The next morning, work resumed, with Spigot #1 doubling its output and Spigot #2 providing a thin stream of water, maybe a gallon an hour. Again another eighth of a mile was gained with the spigots now putting out so much water that even though the buckets were taking up as much water as possible, a small pond was being created at Spigot #1.

The third day showed more improvement as both spigots were dumping out enough water to be carried away. In a hunch, Captain Majewski had even more water dumped on the pathways, making them wider. It seemed where there was paste, the temperatures were lower, if only slightly. At the end of the day the four travelers met with Terri and Captain Majewski, and it was agreed, if they could continue making the same progress for another three days, the path would be roughly a mile long. From there a hut would be created from the muck the nuggets transformed into. The four travelers could hunker down and spend the night at the hut before making a break for to the west at the first sign of dawn. Hopefully reaching the site where the light had been seen. Was it ten miles away? Was it twenty? It might even be fifty.

The Captain's orders were very clear. If there was any question regarding reaching the destination, they were to turn back, and before they were too exhausted and dehydrated to come home. Only a grumpy Hap disagreed, snipping about the physical weakness of his traveling partners. In the allotted three days the hut was constructed and the four prepared for the bracing cold night.

Everyone could see as the four left the hut, heading west. Climbing to the top of SS 222 with several water buckets beside to cool himself with, Captain Majewski could see as the four men shrunk to the size of dots. Finally, after two hours, three of the dots turned back, the fourth... the one in the lead… continued on. "Damn you Hap," mumbled the Captain.

At least the return would be easier as work continued on the path. Considering the potential impending disaster the Captain looked at the ground below and could see Spigot #1 had a pond in front of it and even a trickle heading east, pushing steam into the air. As for Spigot #2, he could see the silver thread of water reaching to the ground where it disappeared. Next to it were two of the children, cupping their hands and tossing water to the side over the golden kernels. Climbing from his perch, he waited for the three to return and tell him what he already knew. The heat had been too much and Gordon had given the word to turn back, but Hap had refused, stubbornly choosing instead to push on.

The meeting was short and to the point, or rather pointless, since Gordon told the Captain exactly that. Hap was convinced they were close, and stated he would not be turning back. That meant either he was dying, dead, or about to connect with the mysterious light. All were bad. Dead or dying and they had lost another member. If he made it by disobeying orders, the Captain looked weak. Asked if they were close to the light, all three were in agreement. No, not at all.

Nodding his head in understanding, the Captain made the decision. No more forays into the heat. Instead the system of carrying the water to the west would be continued. Sort of a great wall in reverse. A great path. If they continued on there current pace, it was a mile or so per week. No, that wasn't right. The winds were usually mild, but could whip up at any moment, and that meant the sections of the path were almost daily being covered with the sharp golden nuggets. Sometimes a sprinkle, others wiping out the path for stretches of ten feet or more.

The next several weeks took on a sameness, from dawn to dusk water was toted down the path, with coordinated groups taking on the roles of working small sections of the path. Better buckets had been fashioned and with the first rays, the crews to work the farthest running ahead to prepare for their day of toting water to the furthest reaches of the colony's expanding realm. Captain Majewski now worried all the time. One sand storm, or rather golden nugget storm would wipe out the path and everyone on it. Something he didn't know if the colony could withstand. The only good news came from the water spigots, which now poured out a stream in each, roughly half the width of the four foot wide spigot. With the added output, a river was slowly burning its way into the ground. It was interesting to watch as the invading water seemed to melt the nuggets before them, sending up steam and leaving a ditch that easily fit the water inside. The spigots, about fifty feet apart, were carving two rivers in parallel to the east as they slowly spread apart. The idea had been broached of digging a ditch to merge the rivers, but the Captain overruled. He wanted to see how they interacted with the environment. After all, a ditch could be carved out whenever needed.

He guessed the rivers were advancing at about four feet a minute. At that rate they would expand over a mile a month, assuming no increase or decrease in pace. But as the water flow from the taps increased it was logical the rate of advance would improve as well. An interesting discovery was that the area between the two streams was becoming more temperate, with colds still cold but not so much and highs that were lower that just outside the span of the two rivers. On a hunch, a small garden was requisitioned between the two rivers. Not that they would need any food grown outside SS 222, which had been stocked with golden nuggets before dumping water on them. The resulting mush was proving very fertile for plant life.

In a strange way, life was beginning to feel more normal on New Earth. Just as on Earth with its four seasons gave a sense of time to ones life, New Earth with its hot days and cold nights, was beginning to develop a rhythm, and the inhabitants of SS 222 were beginning to adopt. It wasn't home yet, but at least it wasn't completely alien any more.

They Never Returned

It was the end of the day, and the final crew – those who worked at trailblazing the end of the path – never returned. The next day all work was halted as sentinels were ordered down the pathway and beyond to determine what had happened. They returned to report no sign of the workers, nor where they had disappeared to. Had a flash sand storm buried them? No, it seemed not. It was bad enough when they came across the body of Hap, dehydrated and looking as if bones wrapped with wrinkled skin. Now six more had been lost on what was being called "The Captain's Folly." Why spend so much time and effort on a path to nowhere when they had ample water around SS 222. Why not focus efforts there when everyone was exhausted, and for what?

The next three days, even though work resumed, little was accomplished – the motivational energy drained from the workers. Then, just as nightfall approached, there they were – the missing six – grinning ear to ear. And when they spoke... it was of Eden, or so it sounded. Lanny Fillmore, Senator Fillmore's son, had landed and started his own water transformer. Smaller than the two beside SS 222, but still... he had a lake, a river, plants, even a small growing grassland around his ship.

How had they reached him? He had appeared an hour or so before nightfall and persuaded the six to make the trek to his oasis, complete with a slowly expanding river which was meandering toward SS 222. He had shut down his northern and southern side streams, focusing on forcing his river toward the east. The trip to his lodgings had almost killed them in the cold, but it was worth the effort. After several days for recovery – and to relax at the amazing green oasis – they had made the return trip.

There was no more talk of resting, as efforts to reach the distant light doubled. Everyone wanted to see the perfect lake, with its surrounding grass and bushes with berries, and trees. Yes, even trees. And then there was the weather. If what the six claimed was true, temperatures the lake were more temperate, almost approaching Earth like. The next day, the crew of six was sent to on Lanny's side so that the two sides might meet up more quickly. After all, no water had to be toted on Lanny's side, just assist in pushing its way toward SS 222. It was a week before Lanny and the six were able to splash water to the path made by SS 222. When the path linked up to Lanny's river and water began to flow down the path, it was cheered as if a meeting of long lost friends as it passed by one worker after another.

It took a few days for the water from Lanny's Oasis to flow down the path and reach SS 222, connecting up with and helping supply the water from Spigot #1. Lanny had arrived much earlier. Upon seeing her son, Dolly realized, she was looking at a different person. What she had left on Earth was an immature boy, a soft layer of blubber encasing his body, and with a constant distant lazy gaze. Now before was her a willowy but strong man, with a firm grip and eyes to match. A small frown escaped Dolly's lips. In some ways he now was like his father. There were many good qualities to the Senator, but not enough she wished such a transformation on her son.

As for Lanny, naturally he was upset. His father had shipped him to what was most certainly a horrible death. But as he glanced around in the glow of lights inside SS 222, the grumbling dissipated before melting away. He was a changed man now, and understood his father had done what was best for him. Though Lanny didn't mention it, Senator Fillmore had even committed murder so that his son would survive. What greater act of love could Lanny ask for?

And where was father? The father and Senator who had saved his life? Dolly was evasive. His rocket ship didn't make it, nor did he. Unsatisfied, Lanny inquired around, and earned little for his efforts. The story of Senator Fillmore – and his absence – became the big secret. Realizing Lanny was intent on answers, the Party of Three, assisted by Jim, met with Lanny. His father had tried to board early, as his ship was low on fuel. The attempt failed, destroying the docking station and he had been left behind. As evidence of their story, Lanny was led to the docking station where it was easy to see the damaged hatches. It all made sense, fit together well.

But even as hands were shaken and Lanny accepted their condolences, something was missing. His father was dead. That was easy to grasp. But the way the Senator's death was presented, no one could look him in the eye... not quite, with the words coming out at times as if forced. For all his laziness, Lanny was his father's son, and so the innate ability to sense when a story was wrong was an inborn talent... and things weren't adding up, not completely. For now... he held his tongue. His mother was alive and so was he. That alone was a miracle, one that he could thank his father for. Still, until he could come to terms with his father's death, remaining at SS 222 was inappropriate. As if he was trespassing on his father's legacy. Lanny chose self imposed exile over reuniting, returning to his private oasis. For now, Lanny would avoid those he had wished for so long to reunite with.

Year One

On Earth, the Gregorian calendar was the standard for tracking time as it passes, logging the day, month, and year with great precision. With Lanny Fillmore joining with SS 222, it was considered by many to be the beginning of New Earth. His arrival made their small band of aliens a community, one with lakes and the ability to grow food outside and under the sun. In short they could live and survive outside the technology bubble of their spaceships. No one knows who said it first, but Lanny's arrival was known as Day One. And with the merging of his river to Spigot #1 the river was dubbed at first the New Nile. But as Spigot #2 continued to gain in strength, they were renamed. The Blue Nile for Spigot #1 and White Nile for Spigot #2. The Blue Nile – with the assistance of Lanny's water transformer – blasted its way East at two miles a month across the low sierra plane as the White Nile dragged along at the relatively slow pace of a mile a month. At the end of the first year they had meandered apart until they were separated by almost five miles of land – barren, except of course for heaps of golden nuggets.

Around SS 222 the community began the process of development as the lands surrounding the space ship were irrigated and vegetables and small fruit trees flourished. It seems the infusion of water, combined with the surrounding expanse of vegetation, reduced the harshness of the weather. Grass, which was originally only survived on Lanny's Oasis, appeared roughly six months after Day One, either from seeds floating down stream, or picked up on a breeze. Regardless of the reason for its arrival, the grounds quickly went from a hodge-podge of plants to manicured gardens with neat rows of vegetables.

Death also continued to follow the colony as any ailment was a potentially fatal, with five more casualties. But births were up as well, as having children was encouraged by the Party of Three, who wanted new bodies to populate the growing fertile lands. The first of the children saved in dining room B were turning eighteen and already three new couples, all pregnant with children, had been welcomed into the community. In addition four more babies were on the way now that food and water seemed more secure.

As the ground around SS 222 became more mature, water was siphoned from the main river, and the land around the space station flourished to a half mile grassy plain. While big in surface area, it was still too fragile to sustain any significant population, with open patches of the sharp golden kernels gleaming throughout the meadow. People began to make the pilgrimage to Lanny's Oasis to marvel at the tall cliffs and the expanding grassland with small trees he had created. A small mud hut was even constructed for those who came stay for the evening, lest they be caught in the heat of the day or cold of night. The thin river that led from Lanny's Oasis to SS 222 now was roughly two feet wide with a thick thatch of grass on each side for most of the distance, pushing out from the river about a foot on each side. When people came for a visit, they would arrive by walking during the day directly through the river, dumping water over their heads or even sitting down if necessary. Those who came were encouraged to toss water on the grass beside the river or the golden kernels that were always about.

These pilgrimages were temporarily stopped when a sandstorm – not a big one, just a dust devil – dumped a blanket of golden kernels atop the river bed for quarter mile. It wasn't more than a few weeks before the river, with the help from SS 222, returned to normal.

To combat future damage to the river, a small group of teens, fourteen or over, were assigned to march up and down the river looking for blockages or other problems, reporting on the expansion of the grass and sightings of new fruit trees or vegetables.

As for the Party of Three, they reigned supreme, having created through luck and hard work a community. Everyone wasn't happy, but then now wasn't the time to complain. The major and most immediate task was finding someone who wanted to be and was capable of being a doctor. Too many people were dying, and researching illnesses on the computer wasn't enough. They needed someone that could complete physical exams and perform surgery. Also, the party picked up a young lieutenant. A sandy haired boy of fifteen named George. He ran messages, took notes at meetings, and generally managed to be under foot. But with his winning smile and boundless energy, no one could stay angry with the precocious George for long.

With his electoral victory, the Captain was the most powerful man on the planet, as recognized by his official title of "President of the New World." But being a rather simple and plain man, he preferred to be called simply Captain. As far as his personal life was concerned, New Earth's leader found himself in a difficult position. Most women were older than him, and of those who weren't, only one claimed the title of single. Now pushing into his late twenties, he was constantly disappointed as the young men plucked off the available girls as they grew into women. What was he to do? At his age, he couldn't very well go to a school dance and explain to girls, "You are too young for me now. But in ten years it will be fine. And oh yeah, don't get married until then."

As it had been in space, school was the main function of SS 222. There would be a need for so many things and soon. Roads, infrastructure, stores, and all the other jobs that keep society alive. To do that New Earth needed an educated population. The first official law passed was related to education and made dropping out of school a crime. Everyone would get a high school diploma. Short staffed and with limited supplies, Jim became the unofficial school principle, working overtime to make sure everything kept moving smoothly.

As for Terri and Gordon, they became teachers. Everything from English to physics to mathematics to social studies and everything in between. Their son Jon was now a teenager and part of the water patrol while Mia – a pre-teen – was a quiet bookish girl. As the year closed the family had a surprise. Terri was pregnant. Their family of four would become five.

All housing was on board SS 222, which due to the curved nature of the ship had more limited space than when weightless. Thanks to the limited passenger list upon departure, there was still sufficient room and SS 222 took on a feel of suspended belief. Inside the space ship there was air conditioning, running water – hot and cold, full bathrooms, and formal bedrooms. And outside? Average daytime highs reached a minimum of one hundred forty or more and below negative forty at night. As the year came to a close, in many ways it seemed as if they were still in space, just hanging on from day to day, with no knowledge of what would come next. They only had two thin rivers edged with some grass and vegetable plants clutching to the riverbank sides as their claim on this planet.

As an indication of how tenuous their grip was on survival, with the approach of the one year anniversary, a graveyard was mapped out. All of the remaining bones, flesh and body parts of those who unknowingly gave their lives so that the other members of SS 222 could live were deposited in graves labeled with their names and affiliations. It was hoped to give closure with a formal ceremony headed by the Captain. But if this was to put their deaths in the rear view mirror, it was a complete failure. The graveyard became the grim reminder of what had been done in order to survive. A sort of perverse memorial to document the evil that had been done. There were grumblings over the ceremony as well. Was it tasteless that the man who had sent all of those people to their graves presided over such an event? The consensus was that it was a huge mistake of ego at worst.

The ceremony was planned as the highlight of the year. But the graveyard ceremony was easily overshadowed a few days later when roaring from the sky in a bright fireball a small rocket landed a mile or so from SS 222. Despite the heat, a dozen or more people rushed to its assistance, and were shocked by what they found. Three people inside, barely alive. Goulish looking and riddled with rickets and scurvy, the passengers were Shirley Abramowitz, Captain Boz, and Senator Larry Fillmore. Inside the stench of dead flesh permeated everything, along with piles of bones and partially gnawed on remains of six people, the food that kept the passengers alive for their trip through the seventh dimension. Dragged back on makeshift sleds, the three were taken to SS 222 and the infirmary.

Upon recognizing the woman, Kevin Abramowitz, current leader of The Fillmore party said, and not with much enthusiasm, "Oh my god… my wife."

Upon seeing the Senator, Dolly Fillmore said coolly and without passion, "Senator. You're home."

Upon realizing he was still alive, Captain Boz said, "Oh god. Oh god-oh god-oh god. I deserve to die."

Years Two To Five

Almost immediately upon his arrival, the talk was of murder. Killing of Senator Fillmore that is. His list of those to die was now legendary and everyone assumed their name had been selected to be put on a rocket bound for Earth and certain death. Bringing the three newcomers back from the edge of death was fairly simple. A steady diet of fruits and vegetables were enough to supply the needed vitamin C and D to their bodies. But for anyone hoping to follow through on their threats were quickly disappointed, as within a week Senator Fillmore secretly relocated to Lanny's Oasis along with Shirley, Captain Boz, Kevin, and Francesca – or Fran – as she was called. An old girlfriend brought along from Earth. Dolly didn't make the trip, nor was she invited.

Within a week, Fran returned to SS 222, complaining the Senator had developed a case of stinky feet. Those who knew her better believed she had developed an aversion to the Senator's poverty. Little was said or heard of the Senator, who was rumored to have slipped into early retirement, spending his days puttering about Lanny's Oasis like an elderly gardener. He could occasionally be seen, bucket in his hand, stumbling about the grassy meadows, searching out dry patches of golden nuggets to deposit the water on.

The rivers Nile, both Blue and White continued on their eastern paths, with the white returning to the Blue, joining forces some fifty miles from SS 222 to become known from there on as simply the Nile. The Captain imagined that if looking down from above, the two Niles might form a shape not unlike an eye. With the river expanding at a pace of three miles per month at a width of ten feet, the Captain commissioned two of the colony's men to replace the teen patrols, ordered to paddle its banks, report on its health, and when possible plant fruit, vegetables, and grass. They had simple boats crafted from small fruit trees, chopped down and strapped together. With the river too large to freeze over at night the men slept on their boats or moored to the bank, surviving on the fruit and vegetables that grew on the banks. Up and down, up and down they went, from SS 222 to the farthest reaches East and back. With every return to the space station, they would meet briefly with the Captain before heading out once more. As the years passed and the river continued its expansion, they became more and more nomads, going weeks and then months between reports.

The rivers now seemed to be rather predictable in their growth, the tip of the river blowing steam into the air as it interacted with virgin golden nuggets, turning them to paste. It was now estimated water fell possibly as far down through the nuggets as thirty feet, creating a solid base for the river bed. Once the nuggets converted to mush, the water, with no leaks to escape through, would push further on its way East.

As time would pass, grass, from seeds in the water or blown by the wind, would take root on the river banks, quickly expanding out to the side a foot or so. It typically took about thirty days after the river first passed before the first sprouts were seen. By the end of the first year, a variety of berries planted themselves in the grass and began to grow. From there, each year onward, the grass would slowly expand out about a foot on each side, converting the nuggets on the surface into fertilizer. If one were to step barefoot on these fringes, the golden nuggets just below the surface would easily cut the feet. In fact, to make the banks safer and more secure, the men who patrolled these waters were to use their paddles to force water onto the banks and create more of the mush like dirt, and plant where barren patches existed beside the river.

By now it was clear, water had a very strong effect on the temperature on New Earth, but as the grass expanded, the effect was multiplied. The clearest example of this phenomenon was the area between the Blue and White Nile rivers. The "eye" as the Captain called it. Here tufts of grass and even small glens grew at a more productive rate, as the two rivers formed a seal that somehow allowed the water in the form of moisturizer to travel inside this strip of land. Temperatures here sometimes were barely more than a hundred twenty in the day and hovered around zero at night. There were even patches in the middle of this barren area where grass somehow found a way to take root. On a hunch, small trenches were cut through the eye, to remarkable effect. Carving a trench every mile or so had a huge effect on the grass, ground, and temperatures. Daytime temperatures dropped to the hundreds and nighttime to around ten. Several of the younger families put forth requests to permanently relocate to the eye and, at least for a short period of time, seeking to expand the trenches and increase the water flow.

The request was denied, but only on a temporary basis. As babies continued to arrive, SS 222 had turned into a large nursery/school. Teachers were needed as were staff to raise the babies. There had been some advances, meager that they were, such as a form of cloth formed from the grass. It wasn't of high quality or good appearance, but was needed to take provide for the growing population. This hit home to a bigger point. The colony was weak and there were so many things that needed creating or fixing. They couldn't allow small groups to go off and live as they wished. Not now, not yet. So while the request was refused, the Captain left open the option for the future. As a consolation and to make sure the people of New Earth didn't think they had elected a dictator, parcels of land were raffled off. Everyone was included, regardless of age and without any charge, and could place a claim on land in the eye, the results were tracked on the ship's computer and certificates printed out on the ship's limited paper supply.

Life inside SS 222 took on a more social tone, as the citizens of New Earth took up trades of various sorts, using vacant spaces in the ship for their businesses. Hair shops, fruit drinks, and others popped up as bartering began to emerge as the unofficial economy. In turn the Captain authorized Angel Heatherborne to take on the role of small claims court judge to magistrate the conflicts began to arise from these unregulated dealings. The most famous early case to go to trial was related to Dolly Fillmore, who to her surprise, Muffin and Cupcake, dogs she assumed were female, had puppies. The case was quickly ended with Dolly granted rights to the puppies, who were claimed to have been sold in return for some small cleaning duties in her cabin on SS 222. They were all Dolly had, at least until she realized that she had too many dogs to tend to, and that they might, through barter, provide her with things she might otherwise not have. That was the beginning of New Earth's love affair between its inhabitants and their dogs.

But the biggest event in the years two through five was the appearance of a waterfall. A mile or so to the north of Lanny's Oasis, on the crumbled slope between the high sierra and low sierra, water began to cascade down. It was easy to identify as the steam poured off the slope as water tumbled down the side. It was the biggest decision of the Captains term. How best to address this strange phenomenon? Should he wait and let nature take its course? Allowing the new source of water to choose its own path, meandering about as water is want to do, or take aggressive action, digging a canal and directing the new water source to the Nile river. The cause for concern was Lanny's Oasis. To be more specific, the Captain didn't trust Senator Fillmore, or that he was finished playing games. The Captain's decision was decisive and final. Take action before the Senator had the opportunity. That was how he had beat the Senator in space, and was the plan again.

To accomplish the feat, the colony utilized its first home grown trade, digging trenches. Much had been learned from building the trenches within the "eye." The tools used were better, as were the ways of handling the heat. Already the small community had developed to the point they could dig a trench a quarter mile long in a day. It took a week to create the trenches that reached the ridge's base, arriving before that water finished its descent to the lower plain. The Captain's swift action was justified when, a few days after the trench was begun, the Senator, Lanny, and Captain Boz were seen futilely trying to make their own canal to the cliff. Even with the advantage of water to help turn the kernels to mush, they were no match for the efficient team of workers from SS 222 who had overwhelming numbers on their side.

The Captain's plan didn't stop at joining up with the water from above. With the connection secured, a scouting team was requisitioned to climb the slope, with several specific directives. It appeared the water was diverting off in many directions as it went down the slope, and the Captain wanted to consolidate them into one major river basin as best possible. Additionally, the scouting team was to identify the source of the water. What was creating this river?

It took some negotiating, and arguing as well, but a team, again lead by Gordon, with Barry and four others, trudged up the cliff side. The selection of Barry was for multiple reasons. Despite not being selected to reside at Lanny's Oasis, he was still known to be loyal to the Fillmore family. No one could determine the source of such affection, but Barry had already gone out of his way on several occasions to create confrontations. Certainly the Senator had never bestowed any kindness on Barry. At times it seemed as if he wasn't so much in favor of Senator Fillmore as against the Party of Three. He'd certainly had several encounters with Gordon, each ending with a formal challenge to settle things physically. It was almost as if a point of honor had been breached.

In more general terms, the fact was, no longer constrained by the limits of polite society, the huge man was on the edge of violence at all times, chasing demons no one else knew of. He was a terror that stomped around the SS 222 intimidating, snarling, and throwing his flabby but amazingly powerful body about. It was hoped that by giving him some direction he might be better controlled, or at least kept out of everyone's way.

It took some doing, but most of the water was channeled to one source, deposited into the canal. The only problem was when Gordon was almost overcome by a landslide. Barry thought it funny. Gordon thought it a potential attempt at murder, though he kept his tongue.

In the spirit of friendship, and hedge his bets, a small amount of water was allowed to divert to Lanny's Oasis. The rivers now properly aligned, Gordon and his team struggled their way to the top of the ridge. Upon reaching the top, they were met with the most amazing sight. A chicken, swimming in the river while calmly clucking. That is until with a squawk it sailed over the side of the cliff. The river was not very deep but fifteen feet wide as it flowed carelessly over the edge of the sierra.

From there it was an easy walk to the source of the river. As they moved forward at first it had all the appearances of their own Nile river. The land to each side started out barren, then small tufts of grass appeared, then more and more before turning into a steady thin blanket of grass on each side with berries scattered here and there beside the water. But from there things became different. Trees. Not just fruit trees, but ferns and oaks, elms and spruce. Not very large, but a whole variety. Where they grew, the grass around them seemed stronger, definitely thicker.

Even the grass was different. Varied in type and texture with thistles in the mix as well. As they moved on further, the thin band of grass and plants widened, from about a foot to three feet and more. A mouse was found nosing about, and then a rabbit. As the band became wider still, daytime temperatures dropped as well. When they first reached the edge of the high sierra, temperatures were higher than the low sierra, maybe by twenty degrees. But as the foliage increased, so too the temperatures dropped, into the one tens in the open but grassy and watery areas, and even lower beside the small shade trees. The night was spent sleeping on the edge of the river, which never came close to freezing over as temperatures dropped to the low teens.

The next day was more of the same as the depth of the growth continued to widen, if only a little, and the variety of plants and trees increased as well. A possum was spotted, and would have run away if possible, but with so little land around, it dropped to its side and played dead. This was quickly followed by a raccoon that took little interest in the small scouting party. The trees looked healthy, some of their thin shoots reaching heights of over ten feet, though still none any wider than a few fingers wide at most. To test their situation, Gordon edged out onto the bed of golden kernels that seemed no different from the ones on the low sierra. Hot and even hotter. He couldn't wait to get back to the safety of the river, splashing into the water before diving in.

Again they slept on the river's bank, temperatures now dipping to no more than the low twenties. Rising with the crack of dawn, they walked steadily until late afternoon. The expansion of growth on each side expanding to thirty to thirty five feet as trees topped over twenty feet in height. And now they could be considered real trees, not just saplings. With the sun beginning to dip in the sky, they passed around a sweeping bend and it came into view. Just as massive as its sister ship in width and length, the letters on its side were quite legible, SS 221. They had reached SS 222's sister ship. Approaching the ship, they were greeted with the chirps of birds, followed by the roar of a lion.

This ship was different from SS 222 in one very obvious way. It had been cracked open as if on a giant hinge and rested in the ground like a huge long arch stretching the length of SS 221. They had almost reached the edge of the ship when a smallish man popped his head out from the greenery and said with enthusiasm, "Hello! I'm Doctor Nimitz. Welcome to the zoo."

Approaching their host, the six travelers couldn't help but look around in awe. The whole expanse around the space ship was lush with grass, greens, and trees. And cool. Somewhere in the range of ninety degrees, maybe less, with a system of sprinklers constantly spraying water about the space ship grounds.

One of the men said, "I want to stay."

Prompting another's, "I ain't leaving."

"Shut your faces," snarled Barry, "Or they'll bury you here, and right quick."

"Welcome," said Doctor Nimitz, "I assume you are from SS 222. My greetings to Senator Fillmore."

Taking the lead, Gordon said, "Um, yeah. Actually he arrived a short time ago. So doctor, what do you have here?"

Waving an arm he replied, "Why as I said, a zoo. Would you like… shall we call it, the grand tour?"

Smiling in return Gordon said, "Sure. Why not."

For the next hour, the smallish Doctor Nimitz showed Gordon and his men the complex insides of SS 221 keeping up a constant dialog. There was the reptile area, complete with alligators. "We have to keep killing them, they get too big… too much effort to maintain. I'd have never thought it, but the tail is quite tasty. Taste just like chicken." The aviary, with birds chirping about. "Hundreds of species. Lost a few, but that was expected. And of course the predatory ones are kept on lock down for now." The bug and insect room, sealed off from all the others. "Any healthy society needs them. And they are a good source of protein." And this was just the start. Elephants – Indian, African, and Congo, rhinos, water buffalo, deer of all kinds. "We must preserve our large species." Lions, tigers, bears, and wolves. "No reason we should be the only predators here." Bobcats, llamas, goats, horses, and on and on. Sheep, cattle – several varieties, goats, lemurs, and kangaroos. In all over a thousand species of animals.

There were so many that SS 221 was built with a special hydraulics system that once landed on New Earth expanded the space station to twice the size of while in flight and allowed all of the living quarters to be usable on New Earth. The hull of the spaceship was now a massive roof that protected the insides, like an airplane hangar chock full of animals. This was in stark contrast to SS 222 where due to the curved nature of the ship only the rooms resting on the ground or nearby were habitable. The expanded format of SS 221 allowed for large, sometimes huge, pens, but with all the animals to be supported, it was crammed tight.

As they passed through the zoo, the touring group stumbled across a few zookeepers making their rounds and feeding the animals. Every time it was the same. When they met the travelers, the women became excited, stopping all their activities either to follow along – despite Doctor Nimitz's admonitions to continue working – or disappeared to, "Tell the others."

Once the tour concluded, the doctor commented, "You look exhausted. Would you like to stay for dinner? We have... um, I don't know. Either it is rabbit or... oh I don't know. Most likely rabbit. After all they breed like... well like rabbits." He chuckled at his joke as his guests stared at each other. A meal with meat... and not human meat. How long had that been?

"Sure!" blurted Gordon as Barry chimed in, "Load us up partner!"

"Well, we didn't plan for you... I don't know. I might have spoken out of turn."

"Doctor," interrupted one of the women who had chosen to informal tag along, "Please... these are our guests. We owe them a meal at the least."

"Do we have enough..."

"Of what rabbit? Enough for a hundred. As you said, they breed like rabbits."

"Yes, I did. But that was a joke. We are the last you know. If we lose a species here it is lost forever."

Smiling the woman said, "We can spare a few rabbits. After all, we feed them to the lions, tigers, and wolves by the dozen."

Dinner was as it turns out a formal affair with Doctor Nimitz revealing a personality that tended toward a control freak, overseeing all activities, ensuring everything was done on schedule, checked off, and verified. The cooking, setting the table, and on and on. The staff numbered only ten, including himself, with eight women and two men. The women gazed dreamy eyed at the men, doing little more with their food than push it around their plates. The men, Doctor Nimitz and his chief assistant, a fat man known as Mr. Davies, chatted about the maintenance of the zoo. It was easy to see how understaffed they were. So much so that it appeared that they had little time to do more than feed the animals.

Tiring of conversation about his daily activities Doctor Nimitz asked, "So tell me, how have you fared since landing? You have what… Three thousand among you?"

"No, more like between three to four hundred."

"What? Three hundred… or four? How can that be?"

"How long have you been here?"

"Oh my. I would guess. I don't know. Six… maybe seven years. Possibly longer."

"Well, we arrived four years ago, or so. When we left, it was by the skin of our teeth."

"Really?"

"Earth was melting down, so were the people. Only were able to save one rockets, and part of the passenger list."

"One rocket? That should hold a thousand."

Gordon looked guiltily around before responding, "Yes. We had… food shortages. Lot of deaths."

"Mmmm, I can imagine. Well, you are here now. In the morning we shall meet and then… we shall see. I guess you will be off then. Yes."

Gordon was slightly taken aback by the comment. He didn't expect upon meeting up with the crew of SS 221 to be given departure orders so quickly, and with such a distant attitude.

"Well Doctor, then... I guess it will be in the morning."

The conversation for the remainder of the meal was light, as if all of the problems of the last decade were no more than a miniseries shown on television. That is until the Doctor and Mr. Davies said their goodnights.

Waiting for the men to depart, the women scuttled the polite conversation for fast chatting gossips, revealing the true nature of the men who ran the zoo. The doctor and his assistant were in a word... nerds, and Doctor Nimitz – as displayed at diner – was a control freak in the extreme. Once they landed, the men acted as if high kings ruling over Nirvana. Two men for eight women, and they were in complete control. In fact to keep themselves cut off from the others, they had only activated two of the six water transformers, enough to keep their small colony alive, but limited enough to so that no one could escape. The women had uncovered the other transformers a few years ago and placed them on the outside of the small refuge, hoping to build a river that would announce their arrival. Their trick had worked, proven out with the arrival of Gordon and his crew.

One of the women interrupted ominously, "Do you have guns?"

"Guns? What are you talking about?"

"Then here. Tossing some acorns, buckeyes, and pine cones on the table she said, "Take these, grab up some rabbits, and take some chickens from the yard as you go, he won't notice. Wait, yes he will, but it won't matter. You'll be gone."

Barry, not in the least eager to leave somewhere that had fresh meat available asked, "What are you babbling about?"

"They never go to bed this early. They headed over toward the lockers… where the guns are kept. Do you guys want a gun fight?" She sounded eager, as if hoping Gordon and his group came prepared to kill Doctor Nimitz and Mr. Davies.

"Um… we don't have guns."

"Aw come on," said Barry, slamming a fist to the table, "We got numbers!"

The women stared at the manical Barry before saying, "Then get going. You got guns back at your ship? Yes. Get some, and come back. Hell, bring an army. Do what you have to, but now? Leave or you might be dead. They're mad I tell you."

In the distance Doctor Nimitz could be heard saying, "I say. Still up?"

Gordon made the decision. "We're outta here."

"But wait," said Barry standing to his feet, always up for a fight, especially if women were involved. It seemed romantic to him.

"No. Stay and fight with what? Toss some rabbit bones at them?"

Within a minute they were gone, seeds tucked in their pockets and three chickens scooped up as they trotted off into the cold. Either the doctor and his assistant weren't very good hunters, or were satisfied with their departure, or never had intensions of killing them. Whatever the reason, Gordon's group made the return to SS 222 without trouble, arriving like Columbus from the new world with his booty. Trees were planted, the chickens laid eggs, and a new meal would soon be on the table; corn.

As for a return to SS 221, an army was in fact organized and sent. But having never assembled such a force, it took six months of preparation, including gathering weapons, storing up food, and assigning ranks and training. It wasn't so much for the battle to come. Captain Majewski joked they likely could have sent Barry with a pistol and a handful of bullets to take control of the zoo. Rather this massive operation was on the advice of Jim, who realized the colony was growing and would soon need a militia, if not a police force. Taking the zoo was a great excuse to begin the process. There were ulterior motives as well. It appeared that Doctor Nimitz was friendly with Senator Fillmore, how good was unknown. Jim, who had met Doctor Nimitz on Earth, was sure the arrival of a military force would be more than sufficient to ensure the doctor's loyalty.

The expedition included twenty armed men and young adults and took over a week to make the journey. Once arrived, it was as expected, with the doctor meekly bowed to the Captain's demands as Jim constantly cited to Doctor Nimitz this was the will of the freely elected government of New Earth. As an added bonus, the men were treated to eight, if not young any more, still good looking women, mostly in their thirties. The union of SS 221 and SS 222 increased the gene pool by ten new unique DNA sets, an important point for a community that was trying to be careful to keep genetic defects from entering the population. Already there was an incestuous cloud over dating as the young had children and were already eying potential mates for their offspring. In return for Doctor Nimitz's loyalty, the Captain listened politely as the doctor listed out plans for the transportation of plants and animals to the low sierra. All of course based upon original plans set out by Senator Fillmore.

As the negotiations extended, it became quite clear Doctor Nimitz and his staff had a problem. Since landing on New Earth, there had been an explosion in the zoo's population of animals. Even working twelve hour days, the current staff was overburdened with tending to the animals, and now meals were no longer served daily, but rather once or twice a week in massive helpings. If more staff wasn't added and soon, the possibility of a complete breakdown was a real concern.

An agreement was made. The Captain would supply workers for the zoo and leave Doctor Nimitz in charge of the zoo – for now. In exchange the doctor promised never to question or challenge the authority of the elected government when it came to the zoo's ownership, including the surrounding facilities. All property, animals, and most importantly – water – were under the official control of the New Earth government. The first such example of this authority was the commissioning by the Captain of trenches to be dug both north and south that would allow water to expand outward onto the upper sierra in hopes of turning the entire tableau into fertile land with plant and animal life throughout the region.

Of special focus were the horses, which now totaled over forty, including ten Arabians. Until some sort of transportation was created that would allow for vehicular travel, horses would be extremely valuable to the colony. When the Captain left, it was with two of the women he hoped to get friendlier with, all ten of the Arabians, and ten men left behind to assist in the zoo and begin preparations for the trench digging project.

As he returned home leading a handsome Arabian, the Captain felt grand. Too much so if you asked Jim. He'd seen many the politician fall from grace, including the Captain. Lurking not far away was former Senator Larry Fillmore, a brilliant politician and ruthless campaigner. The horses were sent off to the "eye" between the Blue and White Nile rivers where grazing land was being developed, with two handlers to ensure their health. This in turn meant the first huts on New Earth would be built in the eye, living quarters for the handlers and a stable for the horses. Further, more water was allocated to the eye to try to remove the sharp golden shards from the ground that could damage the horses hooves and make grazing difficult. All of the horses were to be government property, and once properly broken in either returned to SS 222 available for use, or left on the eye for breeding.

Prior to taking control of the zoo, the small sliver of livable space carved out by the river had been expanding to the point it was becoming a bit cumbersome to manage. But with the horses, arable land seemed to have shrunk considerably. When the first horses were sent to SS 222, what to do with them? Everything was still centralized around the space station. Water, food, shelter. It was Terri who came up with the solution. A sort of a pony express. The horses would make the trip up to SS 221, bringing new workers and returning to SS 222 carrying plants and animals. It was a great way to remind the doctor the government was in charge of the zoo and its contents. Horses could also be sent up and down the Nile to the east, assisting in the reporting of developments of the expanding river.

As the fifth year came to a close, the Captain was fairly happy with his job performance. The amount of usable land was growing, the population was expanding, and food and water were abundant. Not bad for landing on a barren planet with no food, plants, or water. Elections were slated for every six years, or twelve months from now. He was ready, felt he was growing into the position. And with Jim to guide him, he hoped to improve on his performance. His only regret? Eight new women had come into his life. Despite all attempts, none had found him even remotely interesting, almost all having been snatched up soon after arriving at SS 222. What is a man to do? It's not like he could look elsewhere for love. And as more young women grew into adulthood, the quicker it seemed they were married and having children. It seemed as if only he and the moody Barry were single. With Barry, is was easy to understand. Always angry and often violent, what woman wanted that life?

Speaking of children. More housing was going to be needed, and soon. The baby boom currently ongoing was staggering as Terri and Gordon had their second baby since arriving on the planet. But that was encouraged. To survive on New Earth, they needed a community, and that required people, a lot more than the roughly four hundred currently showing up on the census rolls.

Election Year

Jim was worked up over it. So were Terri and Gordon. But the Captain? Not at all. Everything was under control. Even when Shirley Abramowitz showed up asking to file the papers for running for office. The Captain replied confidently, "If you want to run, once you tell me, you're in."

Shaking her head in dismay, Shirley snipped, "I'd expect such an answer from the man who tried to kill Senator Fillmore."

What could be said to that? The Captain smiled amiably as Jim scowled. Waiting for Shirley's departure, Jim grabbed the Captain by a shoulder, pulling his mouth to the Captain's ear. "You ready for an ugly campaign?"

"What? Naw. I've done everyone right."

"Even Senator Fillmore?"

The Captain turned to Jim. "Yup. Even him. He asked for it. All of the voters might be dead today if I'd let him onboard."

"Well, trust me. I know Senator Fillmore. Now you're going to get it. Both barrels. If we don't prepare, we'll be hit by both, and never know it."

Jim as it turned out, was right. Ending his self imposed exile, Senator Fillmore came out swinging. Placards were made from paper obtained from the newly formed paper company, Adams & Co. that put out a whopping ten sheets a day, and the Senator and his staff made sure everyone received or saw a copy. The flyers dredged up everything. Over eight hundred people died on the space station, and entry by XJ1 to the space station had been refused. And that was the start. When two of the Arabians had to be put down because of injuries due to stepping on the golden nuggets, the Captain was painted as rash for sending them to the "eye." When clothing was scarce, why hadn't the Captain made it a priority to expand the sheep herd kept at SS 221? As Jim pointed out and the Captain bitterly agreed too late, he had not done anything along those lines. Following up, the Senator presented a wonderful plan to grow the herd, including plans for a cotton and clothing factory. The Senator was ready to go, but as his advertisement stated, he needed the government's support, and by that he meant the Captain had to approve his plan.

The Captain had no interest in turning the clothing industry, or any industry for that matter, over to man such as the Senator. So he made it clear, he opposed the Senator's plans for the creation of a clothing factory. That was the beginning of the end for Captain Majewski's leadership of New Earth. As the Senator picked apart everything that had gone wrong, or didn't go exactly as planned on New Earth, the Captain was flat footed in his response. Everyone makes mistakes, and somehow the Senator had recorded all of them. When five years of mistakes were added up and presented in total, it seemed much more than expected. Slowly the Senator put doubts in people's minds. Still, the numbers looked good, with an informal poll by Jim showing the Captain holding over two thirds of the votes.

That was until George Smyth entered the race. Barely twenty, for years he had acted as the loyal underling for The Party of Three. But when entering the race, he acted as anything but.

Quietly George had earned the trust of the majority of the colony's young voters, having grown up with them. With striking good looks and a slick tongue, he was able to pick off those who had wavered in the past over their opinion of the Captain, especially those who had lost family members when the oxygen had been withdrawn from dining room A, ending the lives of close to eight hundred people. When the voting day came, just over a hundred votes were tallied. Senator Fillmore earned thirty two votes, less than the Captain's thirty three votes. But with thirty six votes, George Smyth became the newly elected President of New Earth.

Stunned by the loss, at first the Captain refused to congratulate the young man whom he felt had stabbed him in the back. But at Jim's insistence, the offer was made. "You are still a young man," consoled LaBlanc, "Years from now, you will have forgot why you lost, but will be proud you left with your dignity. And so will everyone else."

George, an oversized grin on his face, accepted it with the comment, "Nothing personal Brian – he'd never dared call the Captain that before, no one did – but the better man won. And we both know it. Stick by my side, and maybe I'll find a slot for you."

Where did this smug hatred come from wondered Brian. Ultimately it didn't matter. Still far south of the age of forty, Brian Majewski, former Captain of SS 222, was finished as a politician. He left office with no wife, no children, and no fortune. Of course the Captain would have to abandon his large room on SS 222, that was for the President. What did he have? Nothing. Not even any appreciation for the works he had instituted, including the project to dig canals to the ends of the low sierra – north and south – at a span of every ten miles or closer. Already this project had earned success as the water traveling on some of these north south canals had pushed up to five miles away from the main river, with the results astonishing. Temperatures all around the lower sierra were coming down during the day, and rising closer to freezing at night.

When he awoke the morning of the election, it was in a premium suite with its own private bathroom, including hot and cold water. That night, he fell asleep in a bunk bed with a thin mattress after taking a shower in the community bathroom. The fall had been swift and complete. Worse yet, he had no idea what he would do for work tomorrow once he awoke, or what he would eat. In a final act of betrayal, his secret advisor, Jim LaBlanc, had gleefully accepted an offer to work on George Smyth's staff. When George announced loudly, "No more of this hayseed way of doing things," Jim had responded with an enthusiastic, "Yes sir! We've no room for that, now have we."

Jim always talked of events and how they determined elections. In this case, the only event Brian could see was betrayal. Jim either should have seen this coming, or did and attempted nothing to stop it, or was behind the scheme from the beginning. All were possible, but ultimately it didn't matter. Whichever path had been taken, the final result was Brian's ruin.

Years Six Through Ten

The first event of the George Smyth reign was the Nile reaching the huge basin that would one day become an ocean, possibly millions of years from now. The flow of water had pushed its way to the eastern edge of the low sierra before tumbling over a thousand foot sheer cliff. Upon hearing the news, President Smyth ordered the river blocked to ensure the water remained diverted to the canals. But the order was quickly countermanded when his good friend, the newly married Charlie Hodges, at only eighteen years of age, proposed to let the water drain over the edge. In addition Charlie offered relocating to the basin with his wife and two children to begin the process of developing the land down there. Problem was, the water, as it drifted over the edge, mostly sprayed away into the wind, with hardly any reaching the basin.

Still Charlie was a friend, and that was how George did business. With the land of the "eye" becoming more developed, the growing herd of Arabian horses were removed and the bulk of the land given to friends of George to grow crops and develop a massive sheep farm for food and clothing. Included on site was to be a factory for the production of cotton thread, newly created looms, and even a small clothing department. Those who were not friends of George were requisitioned as factory workers in the name of the state. As for the previous land claims? Their papers were declared invalid by the President. When Justice Angel Heatherborne intervened, stating the deeds were in fact legal and enforceable, President Smyth stated the justice had overstepped his authority, as he had not been approved by the new President. The power struggle ended with Angel retaining his title and responsibilities, but only after agreeing to side with George regarding the deeds and the property of the "eye." In exchange, Angel requested that he be inserted as judge for life. This long term grab for power was denied, replaced with a requirement that the job of Justice be approved by the newly elected President every twelve years.

Despite President Smyth's tendency to help those he liked at the expense of those he didn't know, the colony continued to expand, with the census at year ten equaling slightly more than six hundred total population.

With the Party of Three's fall from grace, Gordon was reduced to working at the factory, as did son Jon and daughter Mia. Terri managed better accommodations working in the child care section of SS 222. Because technically they still were leaders of the Party of Three, George personally considered them enemies of the state and determined to treat them as such. Word was sent to the cotton factory overseer. The Johnsons were not to be promoted or otherwise improved in their job, with the same limitations ordered for Terri. George had risen so high and quickly due to a combination of ruthlessness mixed with the ability to take extreme steps without hesitation if he felt necessary. For all of their mistakes, the Party of Three was still a potent opponent, one George wanted to destroy.

Temperatures continued to improve as the water flowed further through the matrix of manmade troughs carved into the high and low sierras. In the greenest areas surrounding SS 222, during what was now considered winter, temperatures typically raised no more than the nineties while in summer lows could sneak above freezing. The arrival of milder temperatures sparked a housing boom of sorts as people fashioned huts out of the dirt, squatting on the land. This expansion of private housing away from SS 222 was quickly crushed by President Smyth, who declared ownership of all land in the name of the state and ordered the huts knocked to the ground. As further insult and to discourage other non-state approved activity, when the squatters returned to SS 222, they found their private quarters considered abandoned and assumed as property of the state. They were allowed back into the space station, but to units selected by the government and were to be considered governmental housing.

This didn't mean private housing was banned. The squatters had proved it was possible to survive off site. So applying what was becoming known as the rule of "Friends of George," limited tracks of land were allotted out as future weekend homes to those closest to President Smyth.

Upon hearing of George's election as President, Doctor Nimitz made clear his eagerness to work with the new administration. Nimitz didn't like the pushy and cold Captain, who had taken control of his small paradise, not to mention removing his private harem of women. Upon meeting President Smyth, he was dazzled by the young man's good looks and smooth presentation. But the honeymoon was brief... when he discovered a new arrival at the zoo whom George was fond of – a boy of fourteen sent to be trained as a zookeeper – was in fact targeted as his replacement. In his first act of defiance, the doctor released all of the deer into the now expanding canal system of the upper sierra. There was little land for the two herds – that totaled fifty head – to graze on, but their stomping about along with and digging at and fertilizing the grass seemed to help water seep deeper into the ground. With the watery canals stretching as far as ten to twenty miles from SS 221, there was enough foliage for the deer to survive without ravaging the land. As the trees continued to expand in height and the grasslands slowly expanded from the river, the deer had available a few small groves as protection from the late night cold.

To extract revenge for the doctor's behavior, George ordered him dismissed as director of the zoo. But with no competent replacements, combined with the efficient way the doctor managed the zoo, George suffered his first political loss as no one was willing to step into the role. With this defeat, the two space stations became symbolic of developing opposing groups, with SS 222 signifying government and those who used it for their own profit, while SS 221 represented freedom and the common man. Senator Larry Fillmore fell in line with George, saying he, "Liked the cut of his jib," meaning he approved of George's heavy handed ruling style and self centered behavior. As for Brian, he was a drunk. Nothing more, looking for anyone he might borrow from to get a cup of the cheap quality liquor now available in New Earth. Not very tasty, but loaded with alcohol.

After the success of the deer, the conservative Doctor Nimitz released more species into the New Earth environment. Wrens and other small birds, which quickly learned to manage their flights near the ground and water. And the first predators were set free. Foxes, which fed on the overabundant supply of rabbits and mice. Digging into the ground was difficult since they might strike the sharp golden nuggets at any time, but somehow the rabbits and mice and foxes found a way. In an act of hubris, the Arabian horses were relocated to SS 222 and stabled inside the space station, despite the stench they provided. They were to be George's private collection for personal transportation.

As the years passed. another of Captain Majewski's ideas began to show great promise. Lumber farms. Trees were needed for growth, and huge swaths of the "eye" were mapped off for these farms, of course under the control of President George's friends. Even though the trees weren't mature, several of the farms were harvested, with the planks created used for homes. The time had come for the denizens of SS 222 to move out into the world.

One of the first was George's young friend Charlie, who was lowered to the basin with his family after a small green patch was observed growing in the basin. It was agreed that until Charlie was able to develop the land, food would be lowered every week. No matter whatever else happened, Charlie could always lay claim to the fact his was the first private house built. A two story that covered much of the green land and built by workers lowered into the basin for the project.

Food remained abundant on the low sierra as the crops available from the "eye" now included corn, beans, potatoes, and just about any other vegetable you could imagine. And with sheep being slaughtered and chickens and pigs everywhere, meat once again became a staple of everyone's diet. So many sheep in fact that sheepdogs – brought over on SS 221 – became many a herders valued pet.

The deer population continued its expansion, with a few migrating to the lower sierra as small patches of woods began to take hold. But they were only a few as the expanding upper sierra remained better overall for animal life as mature trees began create small pockets of land that could almost be called forests.

As year ten approached, New Earth was conflicted. Every day it seemed the Doctor announced the release of a new plant or animal for everyone's enjoyment, the latest being butterflies. But for every advance made, there was a partition of land or a donation for animals to a friend of George.

As Jim was fond of saying, events have a way of changing things. It was just a doll, hand stitched and with only one eye – made of a button at that. But when George was accused of stealing a doll, a life changing event had occurred.

The Term Of President Fillmore

It got ugly quickly. The woman, or in this case, girl of no more than seventeen, made the accusation. He had stolen her doll. The "he" being President Smyth... George Smyth, now a man in his twenties. What did the doll matter? It wasn't the doll, so much as the damage done to her, done to almost all of the children who boarded SS 222. Most had had lost their parents that day... murdered in the name of necessity. They were a lost generation, almost all of whom had their way of life and anchors as human beings ripped away. It wasn't until years later they were informed of the horror.

Even the way they learned of their loss was horrific. To find out the leaders of their small society; Captain Majewski, Gordon, and Terri Johnson. They had killed their parents. These three, who walked among them, and acted as leaders, were responsible for the huge empty hole in their life. The three would smile at them, helped them in school. Taught right from wrong. All the time knowing they were assassins, murderers, butchers of the worst degree. But no one did anything. Why, for committing these heinous acts, they had been elected leaders of the community. Worse yet were the parents – or single parent – of those few children lucky enough have parents. The kind words they had for the leaders of the Party of Three, the killers who destroyed their lives. And the children of those who didn't lose their parents, trying to console their peers by explaining away what those three villains had done as if acts of charity.

The arrogance of it all. Even the name of their political party; The Party of Three. Brazenly announcing who they were, as if heroes of some sort. There was no coincidence in the fact that when the children of SS 222 turned eighteen, they married and had children. To be sure, marriage was encouraged, a way to strengthen the society and expand the population base. But for many that wasn't the real reason so many new families were created. It had more to with the void… the loss of parents. Much more to do with that. If these lost children couldn't have a mom and dad, then they could at least be one for their children, wiping away the pain by burying themselves in the responsibilities of parenthood.

Because everyone was aware of these damaged souls, the others who survived the massacre of dining room A had sympathy for the parentless children. Some had adopted children, formally and informally, and everyone had gone out of their way to let those disconnected souls know, they were cared about.

But not everyone was always so nice or kind. And when the accusation that President George Smyth had stolen a doll with a missing eye, it hit a nerve. The "she" in this case was Mary Kaplan. Everywhere she went since the first day on SS 222, her doll went with her. To class, meals, even to play with the other children. The doll as everyone knew, was her mother's, passed on to Mary after that fateful day. Although several had offered to take her into their home, Mary refused, stating that when her mother returned, she'd be in trouble. When told of her parent's death, Mary took it badly, stubbornly insisting her mother was coming home.

Mary became the poster child for all that was wrong with this generation. Sad, listless, always searching for something that just wasn't there. She was friendly to all, but had no friends to speak of. Her appearance was simple, with a skirt, tee-shirt, and sandals. She dated a few boys, but never seriously, and had become a sort of community responsibility. Everyone said hello to Mary, and she always replied. In a way she was everyone's daughter or sister. And that made what George Smyth had done so much worse.

He had taken her doll. He denied it of course, but why would Mary lie? It wasn't like her. And her story fit in with rumors about the new President. That he had taken her doll, and that it would be returned to her once she showered certain kindnesses on him. The good part of George was what everyone liked. He was charming and very much so. With a glint in his eye and a smile on his face, the handsome young man looked like what winning was all about. Everything about him was so smooth.

But there was another side to him, and if you knew George, sooner or later it would expose itself. With such close quarters and a limited number of people, just about everyone had seen the other George. Pushy, quick to lose his temper. He didn't like the word no, and could become intractable in his opinions. As for his treatment of women? He was known as a ladies man. Would he take some innocent girls doll? He wasn't considered above that, had a history of a few scraps with girls previously. Nothing serious, just a bit tense. Enough to make the current accusation believable.

And then there was his behavior as President. He had barely won office in a three way race, and his heavy handed manner of inserting the government into everything was grating on everyone, except those few who qualified as a "Friend of George." Already the rumors were starting to be heard. That the elections were to be delayed, and even that they would be postponed indefinitely. There were enough people who had come from planet Earth and lived in the United States to know where this was leading. So when the story of stealing a doll became public, this became the opportunity to remove a potentially dangerous leader.

The backlash was massive, with demands to, at a minimum, bring the President up on harassment charges. If found guilty, a new election would be needed. None of this was in the constitution, for there was no such document. Instead, there was anger, boiling over from years of inside deals, missed opportunities, and biased, one sided decisions made by the government that benefitted a few while being declared in the name of all the people.

Jim LaBlanc, always one to try to find a middle ground, quickly realized the danger of this situation, with rumors of violence already being threatened. He liked George, more than the prickly Brian Majewski. But then everyone liked him. He just seemed unable to control the talent within. Always overreaching when subtlety would do. For example, the squatters. Why throw them off? Why not work with them? Bring them into the system. Land was free and available, and they were willing to work it. But no, George saw this as a challenge to his authority. He was, for all his talent, insecure.

Had Jim LaBlanc gone behind the Captain's back to promote George? No. But neither had he tried to stop the young upstart. It was payback he guessed. Payback for the high handed ways the Captain had dealt with Jim, from their very first conversation over the computer. George always though highly of himself. Not in a loud and boisterous way, rather in a smug, arrogant way. He should have stopped George, or deflected him. It was only a vote or two that cost the Captain a second term. Certainly Jim could have managed that. Something he was a master at. But why should he? He was tired of doing all the work and the Captain getting all the credit. Had he switched sides after the election? Absolutely. Jim was a creature of politics. That is the behavior for the bureaucrats who work behind the scenes. Politics is a job and bureaucrats need an employer.

But how then to defuse this current difficult situation? It was clear George had to go. Things had gotten too ugly. "Events," if you will, had taken over. But to replace him… with who? Jim had hunted down the drunken Brian Majewski, and quickly saw the waste he had become. The conversation had gotten ugly from the beginning as the former Captain accused Jim of selling him out.

"Look at me! Look at me now. I've got nothing. Do you understand, everything is gone."

That immediately hit a nerve with Jim, fed up with the Captain's talent for always thinking of only himself. So Jim replied, "And you don't think I'm in pain. Thirteen years! My wife refuses to even look at me. Even a few feet apart. And why? Because I couldn't save everyone in dining room A. It wasn't possible. But for that I am to be ostracized, ignored… hated."

Brian smiled with glee before saying, "Well Chief of Staff LaBlanc. You wanted me to push the button. Too afraid to do it yourself. Guess what. On that day, events as you like to say… they caught up with you."

With no way possible to reconcile, Jim knew the Party of Three was done. It was Brian who was the star. The others were good role players, but neither Terri nor Gordon had what it took to be leader.

With that basic fact, Jim was left with only one option. Four years into his six year term, President George Smyth, on the private advice of Jim LaBlanc, resigned. He was replaced by former US Senator Larry Fillmore. The announcement went over like a lead balloon. But when the missing doll mysteriously showed up and as the former bombastic Senator took to his roll as meekly as possible, plans for organized protests were quietly diffused.

And what made the Senator, once the most outsized of people you'd ever meet, so humble? He was older, and had suffered several losses over the last decade or so, starting with the failure to board SS 222. No one but the Senator and Captain Boz and Shirley Abramowitz knew of the horror they experienced while circling Earth. Talk was of scavenging off one ship to the next, never sure of their next meal, before stealing a ship with the technology pass over to the seventh dimension. It was a backup rocket, similar to the one Lanny Fillmore had come to New Earth on. With no food, they had done what was necessary. They were alive. Those were the rumors at least. That, and that Captain Boz… when properly motivated, was a demon from hell. If even only one tenth of the stories were true, even Barry couldn't reach to the depths of hell Captain Boz seemed to be able to channel.

The hardest adjustment for President Fillmore was Dolly, who spent her days in the space station with her dogs. She had a thriving puppy business with a shop in SS 222, which in addition to Cupcake and Muffin, held a small variety of cats and dogs donated by the zoo. Upon arriving at New Earth, Senator Fillmore had insulted her in the worst way possible. Leaving her for his girlfriend, only to be embarrassed when she dumped him. As a good politician, he did what was necessary, healing the wound with his wife, explaining this would be best for their son Lanny. Why tell the truth? That once he realized his days as a womanizer were over, Dolly looked a lot better.

As leader, he did amazingly well, holding his ego in check and oversaw a productive two years. The American Declaration of Independence was approved as the law of New Earth, as was the Constitution and Bill or Rights. He was a master statesmen, unlike the Captain who seemed to lurch about in his decision making, randomly addressing this issue before moving on to something else. Nor was he similar to George, who was heavy handed and clumsy. President Fillmore was deft and neat, as if cutting with a scalpel. He reversed the ownership issues of the "eye" properties, returning the land rights to the citizens of New Earth. The government subsidized sheep farm was closed down, with all property allocated out to the people. Instead of limiting what the people could do and where they could live – he made a program of encouraging people to move from SS 222, as long as their housing plans met government requirements, which did not allow huts, insisting on houses made of wood.

Quietly he created the office of Vice President and inserted his son in the position, with the caveat this position would be, going forward, an elected position. These were the best days of his life. With his savvy wife once more by his side and son working under him, he was content to spend his days building the structure that would make sure the community survived into the future.

Under his term, Charlie Hodges and his family were forcibly removed from the basin and the Nile boarded up so that all but a small bit of water was pushed to the trenches. This opened up hundreds of square miles in the upper sierra and lower sierra to growth, becoming lush with trees. Farms were meted out five, ten, twenty, and even more miles away from SS 222. A formal roadway was begun that would stretch from the zoo in the upper sierra to the end of the Nile at the cliff by the basin.

After negotiations with Doctor Nimitz, more birds, bugs, bees, and other animals were released, freeing up space for the Lions, Tigers, and other large animals to roam about the zoo in larger pens. New Earth buzzed with excitement, literally. The weather improved as well, with summer temperatures ranging from the thirties to the one hundreds, and in winter going from zero to seventy where the overgrowth of foliage had taken over. Unlike a short time ago when the only view available of New Earth consisted of a thin river with tufts of grass surrounded by mounds of sharp golden nuggets, many people now lived where the scenery was almost completely the green of grass and leaves combined with the brown of tree trunks.

In a symbolic move, the President announced a City Hall would be created. A large building to house all of the government activities of the expanding community. New Earth was now full of families with six, eight, and ten children. When school ended in the afternoon, the air was pierced with the sounds of children screaming, laughing, and playing about. In the two years he was in office, the population expanded by well over a hundred as the community steadily pushed toward a thousand individuals.

But before that would happen, it was time for a new election. President Fillmore was confident of victory, for both himself and his son. They had brought stability from chaos and firmly planted freedom within the community. What more could he do?

The Next Election

It was a landslide victory one no one expected.
President Fillmore had been defeated, as was his son. The
Vice Presidency fell to Gordon Johnson, who had hoped to
lose. He was so uninterested in the position that he had
forced his wife Terri to be the Presidential hopeful on the
ticket. But she had not won. That victory fell to Captain Brian
Majewski, who at the time the results were announced, was
passed out drunk.

It was easy to explain why President Fillmore had lost.
While XJ1 was sitting on the tarmac awaiting launch, he had
made a death list, and put many voters, or their parents on
that list. Some things are not forgotten, and that was one. The
Captain had killed many on SS 222, but in the view of the
voters, President Fillmore would have killed them all. As to
voting for Terri, it was well known that she was able,
determined, and smart. It was better known that she had
worked under the guidance of Captain Majewski. The
unofficial rallying cry was, "Why get the milk, when you can
get the cow for the same price?" The final tally was President
Fillmore 35 percent, Terri Johnson 6 percent, and Captain
Majewski 59 percent.

Once it was clear the write-in votes had determined victory for Captain Majewski, the problem was – where was he? The obvious locations, Matilda's – a bar and pub, and his bunk at SS 222, were found empty. He was finally located the next day sleeping among the unsheared sheep, snuggling up in the cold against their thick coats. Dragged half unconscious to SS 222 he was given a cup of coffee. It was awful, as was all coffee on New Earth. Grown in the upper sierra it was fairly new, and so bad it was affectionately known as "black ink." When he finally managed to became aware of his surroundings, Terri said softly, "Congratulations Mister President."

"Wha?..."

"The election. You won."

"No. I didn't run," he grumbled before saying brightly, "But I'll have a drink."

"How about some water?"

"Sure, with alcohol would be nice."

"Not a problem. Daniele? Get the President here a glass of water with some alcohol… hold the alcohol."

The pretty girl grinned at the joke, and left saying, "Glass of water."

"No," slurred the Captain, "No… Seriously. I need a drink. My head is pounding."

"What you need sir," said Terri, "Is to sober up. You are back in the saddle so to speak."

"Aaaa, no… You aren't helping. Liquor is quicker as the saying goes."

"Oh yes I am. Once you get back on your feet, you'll be fine. And your first assignment is former President Fillmore. He wants to congratulate you."

"Yes! Let's have a toast… to me. Where is my drink?"

It took an hour before the Captain was sober enough to greet his defeated opponent. President Fillmore was courteous, as was his chief aid, James LaBlanc. They were more than willing to assist in the transfer of power, once the new President felt up to the task. To Terri's and Gordon's surprise Captain Majewski agreed almost immediately to play nice with his hated enemies. It wasn't until President Fillmore and Jim left they found out why. With a loud clatter, the Captain fell to the floor passed out, too exhausted to pretend any more that he was capable of managing his own affairs.

The first months of the new administration were eye opening to Captain Majewski. The depth and breadth of infrastructure President Fillmore had instituted was astounding. It was almost out of intimidation that he approved President Fillmore's recommendation that a Senate be convened. It was proposed to consist of former President Fillmore as head of the Senate, with Jim LaBlanc, Terri Johnson, and Shirley Abramowitz as Senators. Next election, the Senate seats would be filled by popular vote.

The Captain quickly countered with Vice President Gordon as president of the Senate, with Terri Johnson and Lanny Fillmore as Senators. That would give the Captain a two to one advantage in any vote. After considering the offer, President Fillmore agreed, with one condition. He would become New Earth's first cabinet member, Secretary of Interior, answerable to the President. The Captain agreed, with a cap of two years for the Secretary's term. The agreement hammered out, New Earth finally had a government, one filled with experienced officials.

The Party of Three was once more in control, and the Captain again had a reason to wake up in the morning. He didn't trust President Fillmore, but then who did he trust anymore? Terri and Gordon. If it came to a battle between them and President Fillmore and Jim LaBlanc... the Captain knew they had the numerical advantage, but the savvy was with his enemies. What else could he do? He would wake up to his empty life and go to work. After all, something had to change in his life. Not long ago he was just a drunk waiting to die. It was amazing how much had happened while he had been in a stupor. When first elected, New Earth had less than three hundred people and no land to speak of. Now the area cultivated or green on New Earth was as big as a small state with a booming population, crops, and animals roaming about.

One of his first days in office, a notice was received from the zoo. The amount of land in the upper sierra had expanded so quickly a pair of wolves were slated for released into the wild. Scratching his forehead as he read the news, the Captain wondered, was this an omen of things to come?

The Next Six Years

Growth could have been the word for the next six years as both the high and low sierra's cultivated land capacity expanded exponentially during years thirteen through eighteen. With the added arable land came stability to the two tableau's weather. The high sierra became more temperate with highs in the fifties to seventies and lows ranging from the forties to zero or below. The low sierra was more comfortable with highs typically in the seventies to eighties and above with lows in the thirties to forties.

But while the weather stabilized, the same could not be said for society. The upper sierra was developing into a sort of wild west, as young men disappeared up the ridge to trap, dig for gold and other metals, or herd sheep, llamas, and horses and cattle, of which there were both dairy and beef. On the high sierra, away from the confines of the zoo, the law became scarce and living conditions dangerous. Barriers were built around the zoo after a small skirmish with a few of the mountain men that now always seemed to be roaming about. The area around SS 221 earned the title Fort Zooland, sprouting houses and a few ancillary other buildings as it housed over one hundred occupants, becoming the second largest city on New Earth.

Fort Zooland was a most conflicted city. Under the watchful eye of Doctor Nimitz, SS 221 was treated as if a historical relic, always clean and kept up. The hallways lit and the bathrooms with hot and cold water and showers. Computer screens everywhere and private rooms as if out of a modern day upscale Hyatt. And that didn't include the personal touches the original crew had added, such as a cappuccino machine, a toaster. There were also several storage rooms, not large… maybe five by five. For example one was listed as "Golf" on the doorway. Inside were balls, tees, shoes, and thousands of golf clubs. Everything waiting for the first fairway to be created. And all this was surrounded by animals. Bears, lemurs, lions… everything but snakes. The Senator hated snakes.

But once exiting the doors to SS 221, life took on a much less sophisticated atmosphere as Fort Zooland took on more of the feel of Johnsontown, the name of the new community growing up around SS 222. Wooden houses, with streets designed for horses instead of cars. And within a hundred yards a still partially incomplete wall which officially announced the city's edge. And beyond the wall, open land. Lush, green... and dangerous except for the road that led to Johnsontown, which was protected by a lone rider who would escort caravans between the two cities.

As for the much tamer lower sierra, farming became a popular occupation as horses were purchased to till the land and organized farms began to sprout up. The biggest concern was when the dam holding the contents of the Nile from washing over into the basin first cracked, then burst. For months the river spewed unchecked to the basin below as plans were drawn up and executed for a more formal barrier that could control the level and flow of the water to the basin. An unexpected bonus of this project was the discovery that the cliffs, close to sheer, had been populated with an unexpected amount of life. Some small amounts of water had always flowed over the edge of the dam, but it hadn't expected to be significant in volume.

An inspection determined that even the rock on New Earth was rich in nutrients. Further and more surprising was that clumps of grass were growing on the rocky edge, and intermingled with the grass were bird nests. Hundreds of them. Previously it had been theorized that large numbers of birds released had died in the heat and cold. But now it was clear they had migrated to the cliffs where a constant mist made for a pleasant rookery. Further, the water dumped over the edge was slowly converting the basin at the bottom of the cliff into a lush green area. Nothing too big, but the potential could be seen. With the upper and lower sierra becoming painted over in green, talks were of where next to develop the land. Why not the basin? Ultimately such expansion was put off, but it was agreed that a small portion of the Nile should be allocated to flow to the basin below to continue the development.

Space station SS 222 now had an ever fluxuating population with births, deaths, and families expanding out to the now more hospitable weather of New Earth. But like most migrants, once arrived at their initial destination, they tended to move no further. Including the houses building up around SS 222, the population of Johnsontown was approaching five hundred and rapidly climbing. The area was beginning to take on more of the feel of a small town and less a cluster of people clinging onto the crust of a foreign planet. Along those lines building codes were drawn up as to where you could build and the type of structures constructed. For country homes, the requirements were more relaxed, but a plan still had to be submitted and approved, to track the expansion of New Earth if nothing else, not to mention identifying property boundaries. The growing community needed better controls of its land now that people were expanding moving out into it, taking with them growing families, dreams of the future, and a dog and cat or two.

As drawn up by the city planner, and approved by the Senate and President Majewski, the main street, simply called "Main Street," was to pass directly by SS 222 and the partially built City Hall. Plans were for a row of two story buildings with restaurants and businesses on the first floor and private residences above. Also included was a large swath of land segregated off for a school with a public playground and a park. Though not currently on the list of planned construction projects, drawings were created for sewers and sidewalks. Such massive public works require steel or cement, neither of which were currently available.

As for the expansion of land, it was both faster and slower than before. Faster in the sense as the canals slowly filled, the land between the thin strips of water became green with life opening up acre upon acre of new land. And slower because with the addition of so many canals, only so much water was available for each new trench, and so the trenches filled as a painfully slow pace. Add on the farmer's demands for water – especially with no rain water available – and it was easy to see that water was a precious commodity that had to be monitored and rationed out.

The marriage boom continued, with both of Terri and Gordon's oldest children tying the knot. Jon and his new wife chose to move to Fort Zooland for a job tending elephants and rhinos while Mia married a farmer who moved to the furthest reaches of the Nile by the basin to grow wheat. He would be, at least for a time, the only wheat farmer in New Earth. Speaking of events, the most surprising event of Captain Majewski's second term was that Helga LaBlanc reconciled with her husband. It came without warning and held no conditions or other ties. When Jim asked what had changed her mind, she simply put a finger to his lips saying, "Von never complaints or asks prices ven offered a precious gift."

The truth behind the return of Jim LaBlanc's marriage was the result of long and tedious negotiations. Captain Majewski had arranged a series of meetings where it was explained to Helga how Jim had tried to save everyone in dining room A. That is was he, Captain Majewski, who had pushed for the final solution. If she found Jim's behavior odd or unacceptable when they were trying to close the door to dining room A, it was Jim being Jim... too loyal to others and their ideas. In fact she was assured, the idea of getting anyone out of dining room A was Jim's.

On the other side of happiness, the Abramowitz's broke up, Shirley stating as she stormed out, "I could put up with your lazy ass on Earth... but here, you need to do work if you want to be with me."

Kevin's former right hand man in The Fillmore party, Barry, continued on his violent ways, seemly always embroiled in some sort of tiff. With no desire to throw Barry in jail – they didn't even have one – the government came up with a more clever way of disposing of Barry. He was commissioned by the government to be sheriff of the high sierra. It was a win-win situation. Barry was always in trouble in Johnsontown… fights, threats, harassment. The large man held some smoldering anger that apparently could only be released when in combat. For the Captain, who often complained the young men who occupied the high sierra sometimes only understood – or listened to – physical violence, the solution was easy. With a shield to fashioned out of a scrap of metal pinned to his shirt, and a pearl handled colt revolver and several boxes of bullets from storage as his backup… Barry for once seemed rather happy. A gun, a badge, and an excuse to enact violence on others. When the position was offered, Barry swore an oath of loyalty to New Earth's governing body on the spot and within hours was climbing atop his new steed and riding off to the high sierra, eager to establish justice… or just crack some heads. The Captain really didn't care which. He just knew some sort of discipline had to be instilled there, and the brutish Barry was the perfect solution.

The Fillmores appeared content to help manage the government during the week, spending their weekends expanding upon Lanny's Oasis. A large house was constructed on the property, one wing holding President Fillmore and Dolly, and Lanny and his bride Sophia on the other. Even though most of the water from the high sierra was diverted away from their ranch, the effect of being close to the Nile helped make Fillmore Ranch, as they referred to their lands, more fertile, with horses, cattle, sheep, and chickens along with a thousand acres of farmland, though due to labor shortages and patches of the golden nuggets, not all was currently in use.

Oh… and one last event occurred, and it was a big one. The wedding of Brian Majewski to the former Daniele Maynard, who was his former assistant. A young girl, she barely remembered the trip to New Earth. Her father had made it to dining room B due to his technical skills, and thanks to Jim and Helga LaBlanc, her mother escaped the horror of dining room A. Daniele had a bright smile, wonderful personality, and seemed well positioned to ignore her husband's constant black moods, telling him to grow up and lead whenever he came down with a bout of complaints – which was often. Their marriage was the social event of the year with literally everyone on New Earth invited to the event. As he stared out over the mass of people at the wedding reception, the Captain rightly stated with pride that never again would so much of New Earth's total populace be in attendance at one private event at the same time. He was probably right.

As the new election approached, it was looking like a friendly but rousing battle. The Captain made it clear he was up to the challenge for another term while President Fillmore announced his son Lanny would be The Fillmore party candidate. The Captain thought that this would be a rather friendly affair as Lanny wasn't ready for the job – not yet. He was of the opinion President Fillmore was grooming his son for the job to come. Sometime down the road, possibly as soon as the following election, he might be a real challenger. But for the "Election of 18" as this contest was being called, the Captain was confident of victory.

But George Smyth had taught Captain Majewski a worthwhile lesson. He would fight all the way to the finish this time and take nothing for granted. The Fillmore party had an experienced team with President Fillmore, Jim LaBlanc, and Shirley Abramowitz. But by now the Party of Three came with its experience as well and Captain Majewski, Terri, and Gordon were old hands at such things.

What the Captain considered his extra advantage was the energy his marriage brought. It was expected that of the thousand people plus who were now on New Earth, over five hundred would participate in the vote. As both candidates made their final appeals at a podium in downtown Johnsontown, Captain Majewski took a moment to look around. Heady times indeed. He'd done much for the people of New Earth… and was hoping to do more. Would the people let him? He didn't know.

The Election of 18

It was supposed to be a friendly affair. A difference of opinions politely laid out. That was expected. The final result was quite different, starting with President Fillmore's desire to win, egged on by his two top aides; Shirly Abramowitz and Jim LaBlanc, who were spoiling for blood. Jim wanted to crush the Captain for the sins of the past. All of the slights, real and imagined. He had even convinced himself that his protracted separation from Helga had been due to the Captain's incompetence as a leader.

Shirley also wanted to destroy the Captain, but for a different reason. That was who she was. Mean spirited, vicious, and vindictive. She perceived everything as an insult and struck out at everyone. As she saw it, the Captain was an outsider who had kept President Fillmore from his rightful title as leader of New Earth. That and the fact she saw herself as the heir to President Fillmore's throne. As to Lanny, the presumptive candidate? She considered him as a fool, as she was of the opinion of all men. To her, Lanny was a hollow man she would work through until the time came to usurp his authority.

From the time she first set foot on XJ1, that was her opinion... her rightful place. Other than Senator Fillmore, she saw no one competent to challenge her ascent. Not Jim LaBlanc, who the Senator had confided as weak and spineless. And certainly not Lieutenant Majewski as she derisively called the Captain. Always at or near the top of her class, she was a good looking woman. The kind that used an aura of being better than she really was to attract men. She hated to admit it, but Kevin had gotten the best of her. She had married for looks and his rich family history. He had been lazy, greedy, and unfaithful from the very beginning. She'd known it, deep down inside that is. But he was glib and smooth, with a collection of friends she wanted to meet. The kind of people that could advance her career. That was how she'd earned her job with the Senator. But when she realized that all their marriage had were his fading good looks and his desire for her to take care of him, divorce was the only option, and an easy one at that.

She had been twenty five when XJ1 had launched, and was now pushing toward fifty. Never in her wildest dreams did she imagine she would she be this old and not a senior official. Especially in the small population of New Earth. But with the "Election of 18," she saw her chance. Get Lanny Fillmore voted as President, and she was a lock. The next six years she'd bide her time, probing for Lanny's weaknesses and tucking away information that could be used against him. At the same time she'd make herself his most loyal and indispensable aide. Then in the election of 24, she'd pounce. Either through an independent run, or by taking over the Party of Three, she would leave The Fillmore when they needed her most. Then she would crush Lanny like a bug.

But in order to manage her plan, she needed to annihilate the Captain in the current election. Get him out of the way and then through The Fillmore party, crush all new opposition. In 24 it would be her and Lanny. The poor boy wouldn't know what hit him until he was calling her Ms. President. As for President Fillmore? He was already pushing eighty, the age when time starts to win the battle of health. She doubted he would be much of a force after this election. That was the plan, and a good one she thought.

The problem was the Captain. Things were going well in New Earth and the Captain could rightly take credit for the success. Even as President Fillmore reluctantly agreed to turn up the attacks, Lanny couldn't seem to get any traction in chipping away at the Captain's lead. And the Captain didn't give the opportunity, remaining aloof of the activities related to the election. The final vote was crushing, with the Captain getting over eighty percent of the vote. Gordon was once more Vice President with his wife Terri Johnson again voted Senator. The only change was that Lanny's Senatorial position was replaced by Shirley Abramowitz. She now had a base from which to build upon.

Despite the animosity of the election, President Fillmore was offered and accepted another two year term as Secretary of the Interior. Further it was decided that two more Senate seats would be added in the election of 24. When this was noted to President Fillmore, the elderly man leaned over and whispered to the Captain – despite the fact they were alone, "Abramowitz, don't trust her. You watch over my boy Lanny, and I'll make sure you get three of the four Senate seats in 24."

Leary due to the recent election and hostilities, the Captain asked, "What about Jim? Can't he handle this?"

"Jim? Aw, he's good at what he does. Brilliant in fact. Look at you. I'd have chewed you up if not for what he taught you. But, he doesn't have it. By that son, I mean the ability to lead. He could have. Has it in him. But never brought it out. You've got to take some chances to be a leader. Make mistakes and overcome them. Hell. Six years ago you were a worthless drunk. Today? You put my boy in his place. And that's the problem. I see more of you in that girl Shirley than my son. And if I don't do something and fast, he'll never get it."

"So why ask me. You know so much."

"I do, but I also ate and drank too much. I'm getting old. I'm the oldest person on this planet... literally. I might be able to, then again... might not. And I'm too smart a politician to leave this to chance... my health if you will. No, you are the one. My offer stands. You help my boy, and I'll give you three of the four Senate seats. That's the offer."

"Say I do this. How... what? You want him to be President next term?"

"Hell no! But Vice President. That'd be good. That and show him the ropes. How you handle things. You're pretty good at it, if I don't mind saying myself. Show him what you do and why. Jim'll take care of the rest."

The Captain put off an answer, saying he wanted time to think about it. The offer was certainly interesting. But Gordon Johnson was Vice President. He'd have to broach the subject first. Seeing President Fillmore standing with a hand extended, the Captain stood, staring at the hand. Grabbing it he promised, "I'll give it some consideration. And let you know one way or another."

"Good enough, but don't keep me waiting. This Shirley, she's chewing my boy up. She'll do the same to you if you don't get a handle on her."

The Captain nodded in agreement. "True. But I got to get my side aligned on this."

"Smart man. Like I said, you're good at this. Ok, but remember, a secret is only a secret when one person knows. We already got two, and that's too many."

And so the election of 18 ended as so many others before, as the ramp up to the next election cycle.

Two Years Of Turmoil

With the election easily won and his Senate and Secretary of Interior firmly in place, the Captain expected an easy ride for the next term. He was sober, knowledgeable of his role, and had already done it well. Except for Shirley Abramowitz he was familiar with everyone and how they were to behave. And that was the problem.

From the first day Shirley went out of her way to be the problem. She delayed, she wined, she accused. Nothing seemed too petty or pointless. She demanded daily that her agenda be passed, threatened impeachment, screamed and yelled. Any and everything to be a pain, she proved to be a master at complaining. Quickly it became apparent that Gordon, as President of the Senate, was unprepared for such an onslaught. He began to become ill from the stress, not showing up for his duties, leaving Terri and the Captain to fend off the shrieking Shirley.

As the government ground to a halt, society continued on. Barry became the legend of the high sierra, with a shoot first and ask questions later philosophy that was tactically approved by the government. More than one wanted man was brought into Fort Zooland draped over the back of a horse... dead. The Captain made no complaint for the methods used as the population easily pushed past one thousand with the census of twenty showing over twelve hundred people on New Earth. Thanks to Barry, the joke was that families were big, and so were the graveyards.

New Earth only had two approved doctors, one of them being the non practicing Doctor Nimitz. When the Captain tried to authorize two more MD's for training, Shirley worked tirelessly to stop his recommendation, as she always did on any proposal that wasn't hers.

Despite the arrival of Barry, the high sierra remained out of control as troops of young men poured in over tales of wealth and glory. Fort Zooland was quickly becoming just that, a fort, with a small army commissioned to man the completed walls and preserve the zoo. The city was now the only safe haven in the high sierra's modified version of the old wild west.

If the high sierra was becoming more out of control, the opposite was to be said of the lower sierra. As the canals slowly burned their way north and south, opening new expanses to the masses, the population increase continued. Johnsontown got its first three story building in the newly opened City Hall. This was followed by a four story construction a few blocks away complete with a plaque stating it was the tallest building in all of New Earth. There were rumors of a miner finding a trove of ore in the high sierra, but as with all stories about that came from there, they were of questionable value.

With the success in creating a form of paper that could be mass produced, the colony's first newspaper started up. The New Earth Truth, a collection of gossip and announcements along with the story of the day, often detailing the outrageous behavior of Shirley Abramowitz in her battles with the Captain.

The most interesting story the paper occasionally wrote about was of George Smyth, the disgraced President, who now was making a play for the rocket ship that Lanny Fillmore had flown to New Earth. He was lining up support for the opportunity to take the ship to the other side of the basin… about fifty miles from where the Nile was now draining down into the basin, and start another colony. His logic was that with two sources of water pouring into the basin, the entire basin would soon be green and fertile.

Everyone opposed the plan, even Senator Abramowitz, until former President Smyth claimed there were two unused water transformers available for his project. After repeated government denials of their existence, George led Samuel Hobbs, editor in chief of The New Earth Truth, to the back of SS 222, opening a storage bin displaying two such machines. The scandal would take up pages upon pages of the newspaper as Shirely Abramowitz demanded an investigation, asking flatly, "What else is President Majewski hiding?"

Amidst this unfolding drama, one night George stole Lanny Fillmore's space craft, landing it in front of SS 222, and after securing the two newly found water transporters tied to the craft, George soared away to the other side of the basin. Now the Captain had two scandals to manage as everyone questioned why the rocket hadn't been secured and under guard. Foolishness of course, but people were entertained by the story, and the more Samuel Hobbs printed, the more they were drawn into the storyline.

As for the Captain, he was now smart enough as a politician to find a positive in all this. These blunders had happened early in his term. This allowed lots of time to fix things. As to George, the Captain was confident between now and the next election, George would find a way to screw things up. With this thought, the Captain smiled and thought of his former friend, Jim LaBlanc. "Events," Jim would dramatically say, "They have a way of changing things."

Jim's philosophy had been proven true time and again since the first day on SS 222 when the Captain was lucky to come across the list of those to be taken off the space ship and send back to Earth to die. Since then, events had gotten him beat up, thrown out of office, and turned into a drunk. But they also had made him leader of the entire world... several times, and sent him the perfect wife.

When they first landed on New Earth, he worried every day about surviving to the next. Not anymore. Now the Captain was an expert at events, riding them like a Captain sailing his ship upon in rough seas, bouncing among the waves, knowing when they would crest and how to survive the worst. He didn't know where events would take him and New Earth to next. But he was ready... no matter where they led.

Part III – The Diaries of Terri and Mia Johnson

Part IV – The Holiday of Pie Johnson

www.ingramcontent.com/pod-product-compliance
Lightning Source LLC
Chambersburg PA
CBHW060637130626
46555CB00002B/851